DEMON CURSE

LINSEY HALL

For Kitty.

1

BOURBON STREET WAS *DISGUSTING* AT MIDNIGHT.

I sidestepped some beads and puke and peered into a neon-lit bar that sold daiquiris by the bucket.

Nope, no demon in there.

I looked down at my tracking charm and shook it. Damned thing was faulty.

A job for the Council of Demon Slayers had brought me to New Orleans—an otherwise very beautiful city—but of course the demon had headed straight for Bourbon Street. On a Saturday night.

The result was a hunt through masses of drunken humans, all who seemed to think this was their last day on earth, and they were going to live it up with alcoholic day-glow slushies loaded with cheap booze.

Well, it wasn't their last day on earth, but I had to bet they'd wake up tomorrow and wish it had been.

I dodged a tall man who was so wasted that he listed to the left like a ship at sail.

"Hey, pretty lady," he slurred, his bleary eyes meeting mine.

"That's going to be a hard pass." I gave my voice its iciest inflection, but he didn't seem to notice.

Instead, he reached for my hip and squeezed. Hard.

"I didn't say you could touch." I kneed him in the balls, giving it all my strength.

His eyes nearly ejected from his head, and he gave a long keening wail before toppling over.

"Bitch!" his friend shouted.

I turned to him and hissed.

He stumbled backward. "Uh, sorry. Sorry!"

"Morons." Maybe I needed to engage my ghost suit. That would at least allow me to avoid these little irritations, and none of these drunks would notice bumping into someone who they couldn't see.

But then again, I liked teaching assholes a lesson. After all, everyone needed a hobby.

I strode away, dividing my attention between the street around me and the charm in my hand. It vibrated harder the closer I got to my prey, and it was rumbling low right now.

The party heaved around me, people spilling out of bars and onto the street. Wild faces and cups of neon booze filled my vision, along with beads flying from the balconies above.

In the distance, a tall, dark-haired figure caught my eye.

Declan.

My heart leapt, just slightly. Then he turned.

Not Declan.

Not even close.

He wasn't as tall or as handsome; his shoulders weren't as broad. And I'd bet the guy—a thoroughly average human, at that—wasn't half as charming or clever.

Damned Declan had been on my mind ever since we'd parted ways a few days ago. He'd figured out what I was—and promised not to tell—but since I'd created nullification magic within myself, my touch made him sick. That was one of the major downsides of repressing someone's magic—they wanted to puke.

And as much as he wanted to kiss me, becoming physically ill while doing so was a pretty big buzzkill.

Ah, well. I shook away any thought of him and focused on the hunt.

The charm in my hand buzzed hard, and I stopped, peering into the bar next to me. It was dark and dirty, with no neon daiquiri machines. The long bar was filled with slumped-over regulars—people who considered boozing their job rather than an infrequent opportunity to get crazy.

From what I knew of the demon, I wasn't surprised that he would be here.

When they'd sent me on this job, the council had told me that he was an Arokia demon—extremely strong and almost human looking. He specialized in stealing the senses of humans around him, making them blind or deaf. He could keep the senses for his own—thereby making his stronger—or sell them on the black market.

Though I'd normally work only in Magic's Bend, the New Orleans demon slayer was on a well-deserved holiday, so they'd called me in.

I flicked up my hood, igniting the magic in my ghost suit, and slipped into the bar, totally invisible except for the faintest shimmer on the air. Sad sap music was playing on the radio, and I avoided getting too close to the patrons.

As expected, I found the Arokia demon sitting at the edge of the bar, cozied up to a man who was so deep in his cups that he looked like he might fall asleep. The Arokia demon wore an old hoodie to cover his horns, but the rest of him looked almost human, if you ignored the unusually gray pallor to his skin.

He had his arm draped over the man's shoulder, looking for

all the world like he was comforting him after a bad breakup. Magic sparked in the air, so faint that you wouldn't sense it if you didn't know to search for it. It looked like the slightest glitter of energy, traveling from the drunken man to the demon.

I focused on the Arokia with laser precision as I crept forward, drawing a dagger from the ether. Silence was key here, since the demon could have extra strong senses, depending on how many humans he'd stolen from.

I was careful to keep my magical signature repressed. It was stronger since I'd created the nullification magic, almost impossible for me to fully hide. It'd get even worse if I created more permanent magic, which I sure as hell wasn't going to do.

But that was a problem for another day.

Today, I had a demon to catch.

The bastard in question tilted his head to the left, his hoodie shifting with the movement.

Shit.

Before I could throw my dagger, the demon leapt off the stool and ran for it.

"Hey!" The drunk nearly tipped over without the demon to support him.

I raced after my prey, who sprinted toward the back of the bar, shoving chairs and people aside.

I stayed right on his tracks, avoiding any collisions, and plowed out of the bar behind him. The alley was dark and dirty, with the distinct scents of piss and puke. I didn't even want to *think* of what was happening to my boots out here.

The demon sprinted down the alley to my right, fast as a snake.

I turned and raced after him, only able to gain on him by a few feet. Damn, he was fast. My lungs heaved and my muscles burned as I ran, gripping the dagger in my hand.

He was about twenty feet in front of me. When I had a good

line of sight, I hurled the dagger at him. As if he heard it whistling through the air, he veered left to avoid it. The steel plunged into his shoulder, but he didn't make a noise, just flinched and slowed a bit.

I put on a burst of speed to catch him.

At the end of the alley, he veered right onto the street. It was much quieter there, and cleaner. No revelers or cars, just the ancient silence of New Orleans at night.

Exhaustion tugged at me, but I pushed myself faster. The demon sprinted across the street, headed straight for a voodoo shop with wide glass windows. He leapt straight for one, plowing through the glass. It shattered as he smashed into the shop.

I raced in after him, leaping over the broken glass and landing in the darkened shop on silent feet. It was cluttered with all kinds of things, from glass vials of potion to dried alligator heads that stared at me with glassy eyes.

I stopped dead in my tracks, listening for my prey.

He was smart, though, silent as the grave as he crept between the aisles.

When a potion bomb hurtled toward me, I barely caught sight of it in time. I leapt left, diving along the aisle. The glass shattered on the ground behind me, exploding outward.

Clouds of stinging dust and rocks billowed up.

I curled into a ball and covered my head as the shards rained down upon me.

No wonder he'd come in here. Arokia demons didn't have much long-range offensive magic, but a place like this would be full of it.

On hands and knees, I scrambled around the side of the shelf, heading to the spot where the demon should be, given the direction from which the bomb had flown.

Instinct had me looking up just in time to see another bomb

flying at me. Bright blue glass sparkled in the faint light from the street. I lunged forward, managing to get out of the way before the bomb exploded behind me. Icicles shot from it, sharp and fierce.

Perfect weapons, since they melted away from the crime scene almost immediately.

One of them sliced the outside of my thigh. Pain flared, and I winced, looking down. My white blood turned red on contact with my suit, spreading outward slowly.

At least it was a small cut.

Still, it hurt like hell and pissed me off.

I rose to my feet, my gaze going unerringly toward the demon, who was now sprinting for the back door.

Damn, I was so done with this hunt. I needed some dinner and a drink.

"There's no point running," I said.

The demon scoffed and raced out through the door. I sprinted for him, giving it all my speed as I drew a dagger from the ether. As soon as I made it through the back door and into another alley, I spotted the demon.

Carefully, I aimed, then threw, following it up with a second dagger from the ether. Then a third. The demon would dodge when he heard the first blade coming for him, so I'd made sure to cover all my bases, sending a blade in each of the directions that the demon might go.

The first two didn't hit him, but the third did, right in the back and so hard that he stumbled to his knees.

I put on a burst of speed and leapt onto his back, taking him down to the ground. He was fast—and stronger than I expected — scrambling out from under me.

Instead of running, he lunged around, leaping on top of me and slamming me to the pavement. My hood must have fallen off, because he'd had no problem finding me. Quick as a snake, he reached for my throat, his face twisted into an ugly grimace.

Damn, he was faster than an Arokia should be.

Ice cold radiated from his hands, seeping into my skin. Shock spread as my heart thudded hard, and I tried to call another blade from the ether.

"Uh-uh-uh," the demon muttered, an evil grin on his face. "Can't get to the ether when I'm touching you."

What the hell kind of magic was this? The cold was seeping into my bones, but worse, it was blocking my access to my stash of weapons.

Bastard.

I called upon my new nullification magic. It wasn't as strong as a true nullifier's power, but that was good, since the nullification magic would crush all the other magic in my body and make me feel like my soul had been devoured. Still, the nullification magic came in handy at times like these.

I let it fill me, wincing at the emptiness that expanded inside my chest, then pressed my hands to his stomach and pushed it into him. He frowned, his hands faltering.

I pushed harder, envisioning killing his magic, making it go dead inside him. It only worked while I was touching him, but boy, did it *work*. His hands were no longer icy on my neck, and when I reached for the ether, I managed to withdraw a dagger.

This time, I sent it straight into his chest. He gasped, his eyes widening, and I twisted the blade.

"Have I hit your heart?" Sometimes you couldn't tell with demons. "From the way you're gagging, I'm going to guess *yes*."

I kneed him in the stomach, kicking him off me so he tumbled to the ground. Brushing myself off, I climbed to my feet and stood over him, watching him die.

The magic he'd stolen wafted off his body, sparkles in all

shades of silver and white. Would it go back to the people he'd stolen from?

I hoped so. Suddenly waking up blind or deaf would be terrifying.

He took his last breath, and I knelt by his side, patting down his pockets for any kinds of charms or goodies.

I felt a few lumps, one of which turned out to be a small black transport charm.

"Perfect." I pulled it from his pocket and stood, looking down at him.

Sure, the nullification magic had its downsides, but it had saved my life today.

Well, maybe. I'd have probably gotten out of it. I always did.

His body began to disappear, making cleanup easy on me. I'd still be a demon slayer even if I had to clean up after myself, but damn, I was grateful I didn't.

When the demon was gone, I hurled my new transport charm to the ground. A cloud of glittering gray smoke burst upward, and I stepped inside, letting the ether suck me in and pull me through space.

When it spat me out in front of my house in Darklane, I sucked in a relieved breath.

Home sweet home.

Sure, it looked like a haunted mansion that might fall apart at any moment, but it was *mine*.

And Mari's.

We'd worked hard to build a safe, prosperous life for ourselves, and it was going pretty damned well. For the most part. Sure, there were times when we almost died or lost everything we loved—often, actually—but that was life in the magical world.

It was two hours earlier in Magic's Bend, Oregon, and the streets in Darklane were just picking up. Unlike the other neighborhoods in town, residents of Darklane didn't get started until later at night. Mages and shifters and Fae bustled around on the street behind me, heading to bars and shops.

Muscles aching, I climbed the stairs to my front door. Long-held habit had me running my hands over the door frame to disengage the charm that protected the house, and I stepped inside the darkened foyer. It was done up in a Gothic style like the rest of the main house.

"Mari!" I tugged my white leather jacket off and headed left, toward my apartment. "You home?"

"Yeah." Her voice echoed from the right—her apartment.

Everyone who visited had no idea that we owned the town-houses on either side of the main one. The central townhouse was our public workspace when we were doing our blood sorceress side hustle. As for the side townhouses, Mari lived in the right one and I lived in the left.

"Come to my place if you want food!" I shouted.

"Be there in a sec."

I rubbed my neck as I headed down the dark hallway toward the interior door that would lead to my place. We'd built the doors years ago so we wouldn't have to go outside to get to our personal living spaces, and it'd been one of the best investments ever.

Of course, we'd had to enchant the contractor to forget he'd ever built them.

In fairness, we probably hadn't *had* to enchant him, but old habits died hard and we were used to keeping up appearances and our facade. It helped us hide easier. Mostly, though, keeping people at arm's length was a security blanket, and I had no intention of giving it up anytime soon.

I let myself into the apartment, striding through the all-white space. I found it soothing, especially compared to the Gothic chaos of our main house.

Wally waited for me in the kitchen. The black hellcat sat in the sink, his smoky fur wafting upward. Flame red eyes met mine.

"Hey, Wally." I headed toward the little bell on the counter that connected to the Jade Lotus, the Chinese restaurant down the street. It was one of my favorites, and a bit of magic had created a portal through which food could be delivered. I rang the bell twice, for two portions.

Add one more.

I looked at the cat, brows raised. "You want Chinese?"

I'm expanding my palate.

"I didn't see that coming."

Wally was into souls—specifically, eating them. We never discussed it, since I didn't want to know the details, but this could only be a good thing.

"Sure." I rang the bell one more time and looked at him. "Fingers crossed it's not vegetarian."

He grimaced, his little shoulders flinching.

"I hope food is coming soon." Mari's voice preceded her into the kitchen, and she appeared a moment later.

She still wore her black leather fight clothes instead of the plunging black gown that was her normal disguise. The leather was torn and dusty, and her bouffant ponytail was a mess. The black eye makeup that formed a mask over her face was smudged.

She flopped into a chair, looking exhausted.

"Are you just now back from hunting the origin of the orb shards?" I asked.

Mari was hunting a piece of the weapon that had been used to turn our friends to stone last week. We were almost certain they'd been deployed by the same mysterious group in Grim-realm that had sent the necromancer demon to our town.

They wanted to hurt Magic's Bend, and we had no idea why. Or who they were.

We hoped that the shards of glass orb—our only surviving clue—would tell us more.

She nodded, rubbing her eyes. "Still hunting. But those damned things are elusive."

It was no surprise.

I grabbed a half-open bottle of wine. Though I'd prefer a martini and she'd prefer a Manhattan, we saved those for celebratory occasions where we had more energy. I poured two cups, shooting Wally a glance to see if he wanted any.

He nodded.

I arched a brow. "That's new."

I'm in a new phase.

"Of what?"

Renewed kittenhood.

"All right." I poured some red wine into a little saucer.

"You sure you should give him that?" Mari asked.

Wally gave her a light hiss, nothing with real venom, then got to lapping up the wine.

I shrugged. "It's not like he's a real cat." Giving a real cat wine would be totally screwed up. But Wally was a hellcat made of hell smoke and flame who feasted on souls. A little red wine couldn't hurt him.

Mari still frowned.

"Fine, I won't give him tequila."

The hell you won't.

I looked at Wally and winked. He returned to his wine.

A moment later, three white containers of Chinese food appeared on my counter, sent through the portal from the Jade Lotus. I pounced on it, opening the containers and inspecting the contents. Three servings of Mongolian Beef.

"Looks like it's our lucky day." I dumped one into a bowl for Wally, then walked to the counter with the other two.

I passed one to Mari, along with the wooden chopsticks, and sat down to eat. We had stuff to talk about, but as usual, if there was food in the mix, we were scarfing first and chatting later. It'd been ages since I'd eaten, and I knew the same had to be said of Mari.

The first bite of spicy, salty meat tasted like heaven, and I ate quickly, expertly avoiding getting any on my clothes. While I'd gotten used to having blood on them—hazard of the job—I couldn't abide food stains.

Finally sated, I leaned back and picked up my wine.

Before I could speak, Mari pounced. "Have you heard from Declan?"

I groaned, tilting my head back. "You will not let up on that."

"Well, I don't know, it's pretty interesting." She raised her brows and held up her hands, beginning to tick off the relevant points. "One, he knows you are a dragon blood. Two, he seems to like you. A lot. And three, you can't actually touch him without your nullification power making him sick. Which has a really negative effect on point two."

She was right, damn it. All of those points were right, and they all sucked. They made things complicated and messy. Even worse was the fact that I liked him back.

For a moment, I was sucked back in time, to the moment he'd kissed me. My head spun and heat filled me. Warmth spread through my entire body—not just desire, but affection. A feeling of acceptance.

It was intoxicating.

"Well?" Mari's voice dragged me out of the memory. Her tone was so pointed that if it had been an object, it would have killed me.

"Fine. He's called twice."

"And?"

"I ignored them." I didn't tell her about the note. There had been only one. I had a feeling it would be the last. He'd pinned it to the door while I'd watched, wanting to drag him in and kiss him.

But I couldn't.

If I couldn't touch him, the only thing left to do with him was get close. Like, emotionally close. Chatting, etc.

I wasn't up for that. Not with everything on my plate. Or, ever, really. At most, I wanted a physical relationship. With that off the table, it was best to avoid Declan.

Anyway, I had a feeling he was done trying to reach me. Three times in five days—and all of those three times had happened in the first three days. That left two days of nothing, which made it clear that he was moving on.

It was definitely time to switch topics. "So, tell me about the orbs."

She sighed. "Subject changer."

"No idea what you're talking about. Now spill. This is important."

Mari nodded, her expression turning sober. "It is. You're right. Del helped me track the origin of one of the glass shards. I thought it might lead us to Grimrealm, but they pointed somewhere else. That's what she's trying to figure out now, and we'll pick up the hunt tomorrow."

"That sounds promising." Del was a FireSoul, one of the few who shared a soul with a dragon. She was excellent at finding things with her magic, even better than Mari, who had a bit of Seeker talent.

"She's working on it," Mari said. "Hopefully she'll have more by tomorrow."

I lifted a shoulder. "It's a clue, at least."

"I think we need more clues. And faster."

I nodded. This group had tried to hurt Magic's Bend *twice*. We'd stopped them each time, but that didn't mean they were going to up and quit. Hell, if it were me, I'd be even more determined.

"She asked about you, though," Mari said.

My gaze flashed to hers. Even Wally looked her way, his flame red eyes bright.

"What do you mean?" Nerves prickled my skin.

"Just that she noticed you'd been acting weird lately. And that you seem to have new magic."

I swallowed hard. "The nullification power."

She nodded. "She probably asked Cass about it."

Cass was her best friend, and Cass knew that I had the strange power. Along with Nix, they made up a trio and were some of our closest friends.

For us, though, *close friends* meant something entirely different. As in, not close at all. At least, not to the point that we'd ever shared the secrets of our species, even though they'd eventually shared theirs with us.

If the FireSouls knew I could create new magic—a deadly and terrifying power, according to the Order of the Magica— they could eventually figure out we were Dragon Bloods, since pretty much no other species had the ability to create new magic.

While I had faith that the FireSouls would never hurt us, we'd kept that info under wraps for so long that I had no desire to tell anyone else. The only other person we'd told—years ago —had turned us in to the Order of the Magica, our supposed good government. They'd locked us up and tried to use our power for their own.

No way in hell I'd let that happen again.

So, yeah. Our relationship with the FireSouls was fine. Why mess with it?

I shook my head. "Let's worry about it later."

"That's the Aeri I know and love." Mari grinned. She knew I liked to avoid things that I didn't like.

"Well, what can I—"

A harsh alarm blared, pounding at my eardrums. Red and black smoke formed at the ceiling, smelling of fire and decay.

My heart leapt, panic flaring in my chest.

This was no normal red alert.

My attention flashed to Mari. "We're under attack."

Holy fates, demons were *in our house.*

2

MARI AND I LUNGED TO OUR FEET, OUR CHAIRS FLYING BACKWARD. Panic flared in my chest, making my heart beat so hard that it felt like it could break my ribs.

"The enchanted pool," Mari said. "It's coming from there."

Holy fates, she was right.

We'd never had a full black and red alarm before, but this was what happened when the pool beneath our house was attacked. It was our connection with the Council of Demon Slayers, the conduit through which Agatha came to us to deliver news of our upcoming jobs. It was also a source of power for us, allowing us to enhance our blood sorcery spells.

Shit.

I sprinted from the room, shouting over my shoulder, "Come on, Wally!"

Out of the corner of my eye, I saw the cat jerk, then jump off the counter. I never asked for Wally's help—he just showed up when he felt like I might need him.

But if demons were attacking the enchanted pool, we were screwed and would need all the help we could get.

Mari and I sprinted to our workshop. As I ran, I sliced my

finger with my sharp thumbnail, feeling blood well. We entered the quiet workshop, which was dark at this hour, the hearth dead. The shelves were cluttered with ingredients and fragrant herbs hung from the rafters.

However, I had eyes only for the huge wooden table that sat in the middle.

"No one has touched it." Confusion echoed in Mari's voice.

"What the hell?" To get to the sacred pool, an attacker would have to move the table to access the trapdoor beneath.

My heart thundered as I hurried to a corner of the table and let my blood drip onto it. Mari did the same on another corner, and our blood ignited the magic in the spell. The table levitated and drifted to the side of the room.

In unison, we stepped up to the spot on the stone floor where the trapdoor was hidden. We each let a drop of our blood fall onto the stone. It hissed, and the stone door disappeared, revealing stairs that led deep underground.

I listened, but heard nothing from below. "It could be a trap."

"We have to see." Mari drew a sword from the ether.

I drew my dagger, since the stairs were too tight for my mace. I raced down the stairs, keeping my footsteps silent. I considered turning invisible for the advantage, but they'd still be able to see Mari. I didn't want to make her a greater target.

The stone stairs passed quickly beneath my feet as I descended into the ground. I passed the Aerlig vines in seconds, filling my mind with thoughts of how I had no ill intentions. I moved so quickly that the handsy vine didn't even manage to land the usual slap to my ass.

The Lights of Truth let us pass without incident as well.

This was so freaking weird. The Aerlig vines and the Lights of Truth were impenetrable barriers. If someone who had no permission and negative intentions tried to get down here, they'd be trapped.

But there was no one wrapped in the vines or trapped by the Lights of Truth.

For fate's sake, this was bad news.

A moment later, I sprinted into the cavern at the bottom of the stairs.

And into chaos.

Four demons stood near the pool, each at least eight feet tall. Their skin flickered with blue flame, their horns rising twelve inches above their heads. Their attention was directed at the shimmering blue pool in the middle of the cavern. Each of the demons shot a blast of blue fire at the water. The flames danced across the surface, which was rapidly lowering.

Somehow, they were burning away the water of the sacred pool.

Horror devoured me, gnawing at my insides. That shouldn't be possible.

They're cutting off our contact with the Council of Demon Slayers.

I hurled my dagger at the nearest demon, but it melted against his skin. He turned to me, his flaming yellow eyes bright with blood lust.

"Shield!" I cried, drawing mine from the ether.

Mari followed suit, and not a second too soon. The demon shot a massive burst of blue flame at us. I ducked behind the shield, my arm shaking as the flame slammed into it.

"Shit, that's hot," Mari hissed.

Wally sprinted in front of us, and fear chilled my skin. He was running right for the demon who'd shot the blue flame. The small black cat leapt into the air and shot a blast of red flame at the blue. For the briefest moment, the blue flame faded when the red flame hit it.

Then it surged back to life, stronger than ever.

The three other demons were still working on our pool, and it was nearly gone now.

Fates, they were too strong.

"Wally, get out of here!" I shouted.

Wally hissed, then sprinted around to the side, clearly determined to do whatever damage he could.

I didn't move my attention away from the demon, who was still beating us back with his flame. A small lick of it crept toward my leg, which was exposed beneath the shield.

Agony burst when the fire hit me, and I gasped, my stomach turning. It felt like my veins were on fire. From beside me, a sound of pain escaped Mari.

Panic blazed.

These demons were too strong.

I looked at Mari. "Lightning."

She nodded, dark eyes fierce in her pale face. Our weapons would melt on contact, so this was our only hope.

We split up, each of us going in opposite directions, toward the edges of the room. Pain continued to surge through my veins as we ran, a remnant of the demon's attack. I had no idea what he'd done to me with his fire, but I was weakening.

I sucked in a steadying breath and pushed myself harder, determined not to fail Mari. If *either* of us faltered, we'd be dead. The only way out of this was together.

The demon who was shooting fire at us didn't know which one to attack, so he went for me. I grinned viciously, glad to be drawing his attack away from my sister.

This bastard had no idea what was coming at him.

Crouching low, I sprinted to the far side of the cavern. Mari and I needed to get the demons between us. When I reached the far edge, I dragged my sharp thumbnail against my palm. Normally I'd use a blade for this, but I couldn't drop my shield.

Blood welled—just enough for the spell to work--and I

pointed my palm at Mari, who stood at the other end of the room. The demons stood between us, nearly done with their horrible work. They'd turn their killing fire toward us as soon as the pool was gone.

Not if I had anything to say about it.

I called upon the lightning inside me, letting it crackle and burn. It competed with the fire that still roared through my veins, growing more painful with every second that passed.

Had the strange fire demon already delivered a killing blow?

I shoved aside the fear and dragged up the lightning from the bottom of my soul. It rose to the surface, surging toward my bloodied hand. Though I couldn't see her, I knew that Mari did the same. We had this plan of attack worked out to a science by now.

A crack of white lightning burst from my palm, meeting Mari's lightning in the middle. We formed a sparking current of energy, a deadly bar about waist high.

Confidence surged in me. We ran, sprinting toward the demons, making sure to keep them between us. The lightning cut through the first like butter. He shook, falling to the ground as a crisp, blackened shell. We kept going, feeding all of our magic into the bolt of electric energy. I could feel Mari's magic on the air as she forced it into the lightning. It felt like the burn of whiskey on the back of my tongue.

I followed suit, shoving every bit of magic I possessed into the lightning. It crackled fiercely, cutting through two more demons, then the fourth.

They dropped like stones, their blue flame dying as their skin turned gray and black.

As soon as the last one fell, our lightning faded. I couldn't have kept it going for a second more. I sagged against the stone wall, dropping my shield. Across the way, Mari did the same. Her face was so pale that she looked almost dead.

She groaned. "You look like shit."

"You too." The words were quiet as they left my throat.

Wally sprinted toward the demon bodies, his eyes bright.

Before I could blink, he unhinged his jaw and swallowed one whole.

Holy fates!

Was that what he meant by eating souls? Because damn, I did not want to get in his way if he could do that.

"Wally, stop!" I shouted. "We need to search the bodies."

He stopped, shooting me an irritated glare. But it was clear he agreed.

Fire ate me alive from the inside as I dropped to my knees. These demons would disappear any minute now. We didn't have long. I ignored the pain as I crawled toward the demons, the hard, rocky ground cutting into my hands and knees.

Mari did the same, not able to move any faster than I was. I spotted a burn on her leg, as well.

I stopped at the nearest demon body, my eyes going straight for the medallion around his neck.

"Oh, shit." I grabbed the thing off.

It looked just like the one the necromancer demon had worn when he'd come to Magic's Bend to raise an army of the dead two weeks ago. The Oraxia demon had worn one as well.

I shoved the medallion into my pocket, then checked the rest of the demon's pockets.

Empty.

Across the way, Mari moved onto the last demon. I joined her. Wally traded places with me and ate the demon I'd been searching.

"Nothing on this one except the medallion." Dread filled Mari's voice, though it was hard to hear since she was so quiet.

I turned toward the enchanted pool. It wasn't completely

gone. Relief sagged my shoulders. As long as there was some water left, it would replenish.

My gaze caught on a circle of chalk drawn on the floor. I crawled to it, swiping my hand though the white chalk and feeling magic spark.

"What is it?" Mari asked. She still hadn't stood. I wasn't sure she could.

I lifted my fingertips to my nose and sniffed the white powder, then winced. "I think it's some kind of spell that allowed them to get down here without going the normal way."

"It is." Agatha's creaky voice sounded from the pond.

I turned to look. Her spectral form was more faded than normal, no doubt due to the low level of the pond.

"A very rare spell," Agatha said. "We'll find a way to prevent them from entering in the future."

"Good." I didn't like the idea of living on top of something that would draw demons to us. Not that I'd ever move. This was my job. My calling.

"What's wrong with us?" Mari croaked.

Agatha's pale face turned even more serious. "I do not know. A curse of some kind."

Shit. Agatha needed to know these things. There had to be *some* extra benefit to being a demon slayer.

"But you must hurry," she said. "I can see your auras weakening."

I looked away from Agatha. This was the most help she could give.

"Come on, Mir." My veins were truly on fire now. "We need an antidote."

"Yeah." She turned toward me, face pale and eyes stark.

Together, we helped each other rise and stagger toward the stairs. Every step felt like the last one up Mount Everest. Behind us, I could feel Agatha disappear. Hopefully the pool would refill quickly.

"What did that bastard hit us with?" Mari asked.

"No idea." And it scared the shit out of me. Especially since the pain was getting worse and Agatha had no idea what it was.

Talk about bad news.

We staggered up the stairs, moving way too slowly. Eventually, Wally joined us. He walked alongside, his energy flowing into us and giving us strength. The black smoke of his fur wrapped around us, and by the top of the stairs, I swore it was the only thing that had gotten us there.

"Thanks, pal." I gasped, almost unable to speak the words.

Hurry. The fear in his voice chilled me to my bones.

Quick as we could, we staggered to our workshop.

"What will fix this?" Mari asked.

I searched the shelves, heart thundering in my ears. "What's our strongest all-purpose antidote?"

Mari frowned, looking toward the shelves. She pointed up high, to the top self. "Black bottles."

I reached for it, but collapsed, my limbs like jello and my body aflame. Mari went down next to me, slumping against the wall, unable to continue.

"Wally." I could barely speak his name. My heart thundered in my ears.

The hellcat leapt onto the table and onto the shelves, then carefully gripped a black bottle in his jaws. He delivered it to me, then returned to the shelf. I pushed the black bottle to Mari.

She glared at me.

I glared back, then tried to hiss.

She took the potion, her hands shaking as she uncorked it and swigged it back.

A second later, Wally delivered the second bottle. It took all my strength to get it to my lips, and though it tasted like dishwater as I swigged it down, the fire diminished in my veins almost immediately.

I sagged against the wall, letting the antidote get to work.

Wally rubbed his smoky body against my hip, feeling like a strange combo of incorporeal and solid. I scratched his back, which sparked with magic.

Mari thumped her head against the wall. "We're in trouble."

"Yeah." My throat still felt scratchy. "I don't think that cured us."

"Not a chance."

There was still dangerous magic flowing through our veins, a poison that even our strongest antidote hadn't been able to defeat. It was faded now, and much more tolerable, but it was still there.

"Which problem do we deal with first?" Mari held up the medallion she'd taken from one of the demons.

I stared at it, my gaze riveted by the familiar design on the front. I pulled the other medallion from my pocket. Though I knew what I would find when I looked at it, I did so anyway.

The charm stared back at me, taunting.

"They came from Grimrealm." I flipped the medallion over, but it was plain on this side. "Same medallion the necromancer and Oraxia demons were wearing."

"And you said it controls the demon's motions? Makes them do whatever you want them to?"

I nodded. "That's what The Weeds said."

The skinny little mage in Grimrealm was one of the best demon wranglers in the place. I'd only met him once—to question him about the necromancer demon—but if someone wanted to hire a demon, they went to The Weeds.

"So we need to go to Grimrealm."

I nodded at her words, then staggered to my feet. The pain

was still fading from my limbs, but this was a major problem. "First, let's try to figure out what's wrong with us."

I reached down for Mari, and she took my hand. I pulled her to her feet.

"Oh, this sucks." She hobbled to the shelves of ingredients, her gait improving with every step.

I joined her, nearly feeling normal by the time I reached her. At least, I felt no pain. I *could* still feel something wrong with me, however.

We didn't need to talk as we gathered the ingredients for the spell that would help us determine what had cursed us. People came to us for this spell all the time.

This was the first time we'd used it on ourselves, though.

I collected the tools while Mari gathered the potions. Quickly, I found a stone bowl, a silver athame, and a pink crystal from a realm not on earth.

I brought my collection back to the table, which was still pressed up against the wall. We hadn't even bothered to close the trapdoor.

Mari joined me at the table and set three tiny bottles on the wooden surface. Wally jumped up onto the table to watch us, flame red eyes following our every move.

Tension pulled at my skin as we began to work. Mari measured out the glimmering ingredients, pouring precise portions into the bowl. I dropped the crystal in, then stirred the concoction with the silver blade. The final step was to slice our fingertips and let our blood flow into the mixture.

I did mine first, the silver blade cutting deep. Pain flared as white blood dripped into the swirling potion. Mari took the blade and did her own finger. Black blood joined mine, and a poof of blue smoke rose up from the bowl.

Fortunately, these wounds would heal quickly due to an

enchantment. It was necessary, given how many times we cut ourselves.

I held my breath as I watched, waiting for any one of the many signals that would tell us what was in our veins.

The liquid in the bowl turned red.

"Fire," Mari murmured.

The shimmering solution faded from red to black. My heart dropped.

"Fatal." The words were a whisper as they left my throat.

I looked up at Mari, meeting her stark gaze. The blue fire that the demon had hit us with would kill us.

We blinked at each other, speechless, then turned back to the bowl. The liquid within lay still and flat. The black faded to gray.

There were no more clues.

"It's something new," Mari said. "Or rare."

I stepped back from the bowl, testing my strength. I felt fine. Almost back to normal. But I couldn't get away from the fact that something inside me felt different. The curse.

"Let me check the book." I hurried to one of the shelves and picked up a massive leather book.

I turned it over, catching sight of the scrolling golden script. *Curses Most Deadly and Rare.* Mari came to stand by my shoulder as I flipped through the pages, searching for the curse.

It took a few minutes, but I finally I found something that might fit, given what we'd seen in the potion.

Fire Veins Curse.

Quickly, I scanned the text. I could feel Mari reading over my shoulder.

Words like *deadly, days,* and *burning from within* really popped out at me.

"Well, shit. That's not good," she muttered.

"No kidding."

At most, we'd have three days. The curse made fire burn in our veins—or some magical equivalent of it. It would eat us from within, until finally, we succumbed to the pain and decay and died.

"We're holding it off with the antidote," Mari said. "According to the book, we should feel worse now, but we don't. So that should buy us some time."

"Maybe it'll get us a couple days more, but we can't hold it off forever." Not only was the antidote made of incredibly rare ingredients, it was toxic when taken in too great an amount.

I looked toward the top shelf. Two bottles left.

Mari pointed to some tiny text in the book. "Rest will help, too. Keeping our strength up will fight off the potion."

We didn't have a lot of time for rest, but it'd become inevitable, I was sure.

Cursed. Fucking cursed.

Who would do this?

"We need to track the medallion," I said. "Find who cursed us and figure out what the true antidote is."

"Why did they attack our pool, though?"

"So we can't get help, maybe. But we stopped them in time." If they'd succeeded, we'd have no way to access the Council of Demon Slayers. They'd have to figure out something was wrong and come find us.

My mind spun. "But the real question is...how did they know we worked for the Council of Demon Slayers? And why did they come for us?"

Mari nodded. "Only one way to find out. We're going to Grimrealm."

3

————

A HALF HOUR LATER, MARI AND I STOOD AT THE ENTRANCE TO Fairlight Alley. In a cruel twist of fate, the entrance to Grimrealm was on the same side of town as our home in Darklane.

When we'd escaped Grimrealm, we'd wanted nothing more than to get as far away as possible. That hadn't been in the cards, though, since the council had wanted us to protect Magic's Bend as the resident demon slayers.

So we'd gotten our disguises and set up shop.

Now we were back.

Both of us.

I'd tried to convince Mari not to come. It was dangerous for both of us to go back, considering how we could be used against each other if we were caught by our family. I'd do anything to spare her, including creating dark magic.

"I know you're pissed I'm coming, but get over it." She flipped her dark cloak up over her head, hiding her face.

"Not pissed, just worried."

"It's too dangerous to go alone. And I'm done being afraid of our past. Anyway, the cure might be down there, and we don't know how long we have."

And that was the sticking point. We might be dead in a couple hours anyway. Even now, I could feel the slightest bit of heat in my veins. The fire was rising again.

"I'll come get you if you don't report back in two hours," Claire said.

I turned back to glance at our friend. Her straight dark hair was pulled back in a ponytail, and she wore her fighting leathers.

When we'd called her, she'd been at Potions & Pastilles, having just closed up the cafe for the night. She'd been about to head out on a demon hunt for the Order of the Magica—she was a mercenary who occasionally did jobs for them, so she wasn't dissimilar from us in that respect.

But now, she was our backup. Since Claire occasionally did jobs in Grimrealm, she was the most qualified to be our safety net in case we didn't return. She still didn't know we were Dragon Bloods, but she knew we were weird and didn't care. And if she had to rescue us, I trusted her with the secret, since she might figure it out.

"Remember to check in when you get back," she said.

I nodded, wanting to hug her in thanks.

What was with me lately, wanting to hug people?

It was weird.

I shoved the thought aside and pulled a small vial of potion from my pocket. I swigged it back, feeling the dark magic inside me swell outward. It didn't grow—I definitely didn't want that—it just became more apparent. The dark magic that I possessed was a remnant of my upbringing in one of the most horrible parts of the world. Mari had it, too.

In cases like this, it would help us blend in. We'd need a dark magic signature to throw the denizens of Grimrealm off the scent.

I glanced at Mari. She pulled her vial out from her cleavage, then drank it quickly.

Whereas my dark magic smelled faintly of wet dog, Mari's smelled a bit fishy. Not overwhelming, but not nice either.

Because we were headed back into Grimrealm, Mari had insisted on wearing her Elvira getup. It was her usual disguise for our blood sorcery work. The plunging black dress, black bouffant hair, and massive sweep of dark makeup made her totally indistinguishable from the girl she'd once been.

No one in Grimrealm would recognize her.

Her one concession to the danger of the situation was the black combat boots she wore beneath the long dress. Normally, she'd go for midnight stilettos. She was a pretty mean fighter in those too—demons really had to watch out for their eyes—but the boots would make running easier.

And while we didn't run from much in life, we'd both be willing to run from Grimrealm once we had our answers.

I, for one, stuck to my ghost suit. I'd need the possible invisibility. I still wore a dark cloak, however, and flipped that up over my face.

I gave Claire one last look. "Thanks for having our backs."

"Always."

Before I'd left my house, I'd put a note for Declan on the counter. If we didn't return and something happened to Claire, Wally was instructed to make sure Declan got the note.

It was mostly a come-save-my-ass note, but I'd kinda wanted to draw a heart on it.

I'd resisted, of course.

For one, it was too sappy.

For another, it was a terrible idea.

We left Claire at the entrance to the alley, and I strode down the clean, narrow street. The cleanliness was strange, primarily since we were between Darklane and the Historic District. The heavy weekend partying that went on in both of those places meant that all the local alleys smelled of pee.

But this alley had a repelling charm that kept the drunks out, hence the cleanliness.

I glanced at Mari, catching sight of her pale face beneath the cloak. I squeezed her shoulder, remembering what I'd felt the first time I'd come back to Grimrealm. Hell, my insides were still freaking out over this.

At my touch, Mari winced just slightly.

Shit.

My nullification magic. It was making her sick. I withdrew my hand.

"It'll be okay," I said.

"If death weren't the alternative, I'd listen to this repelling charm and get the hell out of here."

Yeah, I had to agree with that. It felt like hell.

We reached the end of the short alley, and I pressed my palm against the brick wall. I pushed hard, and my hand sank into the stone. I shoved my foot through next, finally managing to walk through the wall. It felt like making my way through viscous goo, but I appeared on the other side, clean and unharmed.

Mari followed, popping out beside me. "Weird."

"No kidding." The alley on this side was just as clean and boring. We approached the far end, and I stopped in front of the wall.

"What next?" Mari asked.

I pointed to a spot behind me. "Get ready for a trapdoor to open right there. Then we walk down a passage and hope the protections have not changed since I was here last."

Mari raised her hand, her fingers crossed.

She tucked herself back against the wall while I studied the brick surface in front of me. Last time I'd been here, Claire had done this part. But I'd memorized her motions. The pattern returned to my mind, and I pressed my fingertips to different bricks, repeating the order that Claire had shown me.

Magic swelled on the air as stone scraped against stone. I turned around, looking at the ground.

A hole opened up, a gaping square that belched black magic.

"That's it." I approached, staring down. "Just jump."

I didn't wait—I couldn't. The tension was too great. I stepped off the ledge and let myself fall into the hole. I plummeted, my stomach heaving upward. Near the bottom, magic slowed my descent, and I landed gracefully.

Mari followed immediately. She'd never been one to shrink from a challenge, even a terrifying one.

I turned to face the tunnel that stretched away from us. Dark magic filled the space, smelling of rotten eggs and sewage. Green-flame torches burned along the walls, illuminating the flat ground of the tunnel.

I stared at it. "Shit."

Mari looked toward me. "What?"

I pointed to the flat ground. "When I was here last, the floor of the tunnel had a mound upon which you could walk. It helped you avoid the flame charm that would light you up for trespassing."

"So we don't know what the new protection charm is."

"Nope." I searched the tunnel for any clues, but spotted nothing. "We'll just have to go slow."

Mari drew a shield from the ether, and I followed suit. A moment later, Wally appeared at my side, slinking along.

"Here for the fun?"

And the souls.

I shrugged, just glad he was here.

Tension prickled across my skin as we crept down the passage. Dark magic roiled in the air, a threat that I couldn't ignore.

When the first icicle shot from the side wall, I was too slow. It nearly pierced my side.

Wally leapt up, shooting a blast of flame at the ice and melting it right before it hit me. His fire warmed my side, nearly burning.

"Thanks." I smooshed up against Mari, directing my shield toward the side. She did the same.

We moved forward, our steps triggering the magic. Icicles shot, one after the other. They clanged against our shields, shaking my arms with every blow.

Wally melted as many as he could, but it was impossible for him to keep up.

"Faster," Mari said.

I hurried alongside her, my arms aching from holding the shield.

Up ahead, the ice flew from all sections of the walls. Even with the shields, some would hit us in the legs.

This wouldn't work. Our shields were too small, and Wally couldn't get them all.

"Hang on." I stopped. "This way."

I shuffled toward the closest wall, and she followed. Every inch closer meant that the icicles hit my shield with more force. My arms were nearly dead.

"You better have a plan," Mari muttered. "Because I'm about to drop this shield and become an icy shish kebab."

"I do." Kind of. Sort of.

I reached the wall and pressed my hand to the rough stone, calling upon my nullification magic and feeding it into the wall.

At first, nothing happened. I tried harder, calling it up from the depths of my soul. If I was going to live without touching anyone, then this magic had better come in handy.

This time, the power surged from me. In midair, the icicles slowed. They didn't stop entirely, but Wally was able to leap into the air and kick one away with his feet. Mari reached out and batted one to the ground.

"Nice."

"Yeah. Let's go before I lose it." This magic could be a serious drain on me.

We walked forward, and I kept my hand pressed against the stone, dragging it along and feeding my magic into it. Mari swatted the icicles out of our way as we progressed.

Finally, we reached the end, and I withdrew my hand.

The icicles dropped, but my attention was on the enormous cavern in front of us. It was the size of multiple football fields, sprawled outward with a bustling hub of activity and dark magic. Quickly, I stashed my shield in the ether. Mari did the same.

We didn't need people seeing that we hadn't known how to get past the protection charms. If you didn't know, you shouldn't survive them. And if you somehow managed to, then you definitely weren't invited here.

The stench of Grimrealm rolled out toward us, followed by the feeling of a gut-punch that nearly bowled me over. Mari flinched, too.

"Ugh, that's new." I searched for the creature that was giving off that particular magical signature, but saw no one.

Mari's wide eyes were glued to the hustle and bustle of Grimrealm. I couldn't blame her.

This was only my second time seeing it since childhood, and it was freaky.

The main chamber was the same as it had been—a massive open-air market filled with black fabric stalls and hundreds of tables. Everything from potions to shrunken heads were sold here. Signs floated in the air above the stalls, advertising their wares. *Magick Most Mighty* and *Poisonous Perilous Potions.*

They'd be cute names if not for the reek of dark magic that

made the situation very clear. This stuff was evil, and those peddling it were proud.

"We need to find The Weeds," I said. "But I've no idea where he'll be."

"A fortune-teller or seer, maybe?"

I nodded. There had to be one in the market. We could go back to the library where I'd first learned about The Weeds's location, but I'd rather try this first. Less dangerous.

I stepped forward, and a twinge of fiery pain shot through my veins. I gasped.

"What is it?" Concern shadowed Mari's voice.

"The fire. I feel it."

"Me too. On and off."

"No time to waste, then." I reached for her hand so we didn't get separated. At the last minute, I remembered my nullifying power and grabbed the edge of her cloak.

I led the way through the bustling stalls, walking quickly and without making eye contact. My hood made it easy, and I kept my attention on the stall wares.

When I finally spotted a seer sitting at a table in the middle of the market, I pointed. "Let's try her."

We threaded our way through the crowd, headed for the beautiful woman sitting inside a simple tent. The sign above her head read *Fortune & Seer Work.*

At some point, Wally disappeared, but it was for the best. We didn't need to draw any attention, and he was pretty interesting. The woman's gaze flashed toward us, as if she knew to expect us. Her eyes glittered an emerald green like her hair, and her beautiful brown skin glowed with an internal light.

As we approached, her magic didn't feel dark. Not even a little bit.

I frowned. What was she doing here if she didn't have dark magic?

And why did the residents tolerate it?

"Maybe it's a good thing," Mari whispered, as if she'd read my mind. She hadn't, but it was obvious that we were having the same thoughts. "She won't lie."

That wasn't a guarantee, but this woman had her reasons for being here, just like us.

I stopped in front of her table. She wore a simple green dress that matched her hair and flowed like water over her curves. The cloak over her shoulders was a rich green velvet.

What a weird woman to be in Grimrealm.

"Are you open for business?" I asked.

She opened her arms wide, her smile welcoming. "But of course."

We sat on the two tiny stools in front of her. There was no crystal ball or cup of tea in front of her—none of the usual fortune telling stuff. Which meant she was probably a seer, a supernatural capable of plucking information from the ether. Not all information, but some of it.

"What can I do for you?" she asked.

"We're looking for a guy named The Weeds."

She frowned. "That weasel?"

"The very same. Any idea where he is?"

She flattened the frown from her face and shrugged, seeming bored. "No. But I can find him."

"That'd be great." I glanced at Mari, who looked hopeful.

The woman closed her eyes, and her magic surged. There was a bit of darkness to it. I could sense it now that I was close. A bit like mine, really.

Finally, she opened her eyes. "You'll find him in his apartment off of Derrigo Street, at number twelve." She pointed to the right. "At the back of Grimrealm."

Fear chilled my skin. We hadn't lived off of Derrigo Street, but we'd lived close. Mari gripped my knee, holding tight despite the nausea that touching me must cause her.

"Do you know anything else about him?" I asked.

"Only that he's in over his head, providing demons to someone who is much stronger than he is."

"Who?" My voice snapped with interest.

"I can't see that. He's shielded. But The Weeds has been busy supplying him with demons, and it's getting dicey."

"How dicey?" Mari asked.

She shrugged. "Don't know. I'm just getting that feeling."

I nodded. "Thanks. What'll it be?"

"Three hundred."

Mari pulled the money from her cloak and handed it over.

I stood, but bent down. "You want to be here, right?" I wanted to make sure she wasn't being trafficked.

The woman's eyes flashed with irritation, then understanding. "Yeah. I've got my reasons."

I nodded and straightened. I believed her. She didn't sound coerced, and her reaction had seemed genuine.

Mari and I left, cutting through the crowd as quickly as we could. We headed for the less populated area in the back, toward our old neighborhood.

"Did you come this way last time you were here?" Mari asked.

"No." Just thinking about it sent a shiver through me.

Aunt and Uncle still had to live in Grimrealm. There was no reason they wouldn't.

But that didn't mean we'd run into them. And if we did, we could always kick their asses. I wouldn't feel a bit of guilt over that.

Finally, we reached the edge of the market. It was quieter, though bigger shops and casinos were built into the sides of the cavern. Doormen stood outside of most of them, species that I'd never seen before. Most of them looked built for fighting, though, with big muscles and powerful magic that filled the air around them.

My gaze moved unerringly toward Derrigo Street. The name was carved into the wall of the tunnel that made up the street, and it was dark inside.

"Not a nice part of town," Mari said.

"No, it never was."

Together, we stepped into the tunnel.

We weren't there to confront our past, but I couldn't convince my flight-or-fight reflex to chill out. It wasn't sure what it wanted to do—both, probably.

We stuck side by side as we strode down the darkened street. The lights were dim, flickering street lamps that were running low on power. The doorways that led off the tunnel were all shut tight—apartments that wanted no visitors. Just like our own had been.

In the distance, a shadow loomed. Probably a big man, from the look of him.

Next to me, Mari flinched. I wasn't far behind her. When I caught sight of how he walked, I stiffened. His gait was familiar. A slight limp.

He neared us, getting closer and closer until I could spot his muddy eyes and squashed nose.

The familiar fear surged as the memories rose. A beating. Another beating.

I'd seen this man last time I was here.

He'd been our jailer.

A hired gun our aunt had employed to make sure we didn't escape after our first few attempts.

Last time, I'd hidden in my ghost suit, letting the man pass me and Declan by.

Not this time. Rage fought with the fear. I'd had my chance to cower, and I'd taken it.

Not again.

I shoved Mari back. "Stay here."

She was frozen with terror, her eyes wide as she stared at the man, who was only about ten feet away.

"Don't," she whispered. "He'll kill you."

4

"Not if I kill him first." I yanked up the hood on my ghost suit, invisibility cloaking me.

Then I charged.

Rage lit a fire in my chest as memories crashed into my mind. For years, this man had denied us food, light, and delivered beatings any time we didn't comply. Images of him wailing on Mari flashed in my mind, and I just couldn't take it.

A psychologist might say that a lot of my fear had to do with never coming back to confront my past and put it to bed.

Well, I was willing to put this part of it to bed.

"Where are you?" His voice rumbled out, sending a shiver of fear scraping across my nerve endings. "I would sense that magic anywhere."

Oh, shit.

He recognized us, despite our disguises.

Of course. We'd amplified the dark magic that had cloaked us while we'd lived here.

No wonder he recognized it. He'd loved torturing us.

Well, I would happily return the favor.

I drew my mace from the ether and swung it hard as I

neared, aiming for his head. The spiked ball flew through the air, right at his thick skull.

But he was fast.

Oh, so fast. I'd forgotten how fast. He'd been the perfect jailer because of it. We'd never caught him.

He dodged low, avoiding the weapon that he couldn't even see. Because it was attached to me while I was invisible, he had no way of seeing it.

Yet somehow, he'd dodged it perfectly.

He laughed, an ugly sound. "Sweet little Dragon Blood, come back for more?"

I nearly gagged at the words, rage lighting in my chest. I'd have to be faster. He darted toward me, and I dived left. He could sense me somehow, and I needed to stay ahead of him.

I banished my mace back to the ether and called upon a dagger, whirling to face him. He stood between Mari and me, staring at her. She looked at him, a stark expression on her face, then bared her teeth, ready to fight.

She was just as scared as I'd been the first time I'd seen him, when I'd hidden myself like a coward. But she'd fight.

I threw my dagger at his back, aiming right for the biggest part. It sank into the flesh, but he just grunted.

Shit, he was strong.

I drew another dagger, but he staggered toward Mari.

Why the hell was he going for her?

A memory flashed.

She'd been his favorite to beat. Rage like I'd never known lit in my chest.

"Hey! Dick weasel," I called.

He turned to me, face red and expression thunderous. His eyes darted as he searched for me.

"Yes, I'm talking to you, pea brain." I threw another dagger, but he managed to dodge this one, moving so fast I could barely see him.

As I recalled, his range for lightning-fast movement was only a few feet, and I was far enough away that I'd have a couple seconds notice. But if he got close to me, I was dead.

From behind him, Mari raised her bloody hand. The black liquid glinted in the light, and the signal was clear.

He was too fast for my blades, but he couldn't escape our lightning. Not as long as we had him trapped between us in this tunnel.

Quickly, I drew a dagger and sliced my palm, raising my hand. I called upon the lightning within me for the second time that night. Mari and I had always fought best as a team.

Though I was exhausted and the fire curse dragged at me, the lightning burst to the surface. Fear and desperation were fantastic fuels for magic. I yanked my hood off so Mari could see me.

Lightning cracked from Mari's palm, two electric streams from our hands, joining in the middle.

Our nameless jailer was only a few feet to the left, the faint glow of the lightning shining upon his ugly face.

Together, we sprinted left, dragging the bar of lightning along. He darted out of the way, but we caught him by the wall. There was nowhere left for him to run.

When the lightning cut into his body, making him shake and his skin turn black, satisfaction welled inside me. He dropped hard to the ground, and we lowered our lightning stream, making sure he was dead.

A dark grin stretched across Mari's face, satisfaction following in its wake. When we were sure he was dead, we approached on swift feet, meeting in the middle and staring down at his body. We'd kept the lightning on him so long—

probably too long—that he'd turned crispy and black, like something burned on the grill.

"Bastard," Mari muttered.

"But god, that felt good." We'd killed our past. Not our whole past, but an ugly chunk of it. I was glad I'd done it with her. Bonding, Dragon Blood style.

I took a half second to enjoy the sight, then looked up at Mari. "We'd better get a move on. That was some dangerous magic to use here."

She nodded, her expression turning stark again. In all my life, I'd never seen anyone use conjoined lightning magic like ours. Probably because we'd invented it while living here. I didn't know what—if any—surveillance Aunt might have on this area, but I didn't want to run into her before we got a cure for this fire vein curse. I didn't want to run into her ever, actually.

Together, we hurried away from the body.

We were nearly toward the end of the street by the time I saw number twelve. The door was partially open, the interior dark.

"Shit," Mari muttered.

Dread filled me as I approached. An open door was weird on a street where every other door was closed. Especially when we'd just committed murder. Was The Weeds watching us? Had he run for it?

"I'll go first." I flipped my hood up, though it wouldn't do me a ton of good if he was spying on us from inside.

Silently, I approached, sniffing at the air. I got no hint of dark magic. Nothing out of the ordinary, at least.

Carefully, I pushed the door open, braced for an attack.

None came.

Light from the tunnel flooded into the apartment, shining on the body in the middle of the floor. Brilliant green hair gleamed. The air felt stale and empty.

Shit.

Quietly, I crept in, searching for an attacker. Who had done this?

A quick scan of the small, one-room space revealed that it was empty. Except for Weeds, who was definitely dead, considering that he was missing his heart. There was nothing but a gaping hole in the middle of his chest. Parts of his skin were blackened, as if he'd been hit with electricity.

I turned back to Mari, who was keeping a lookout on the hall. "It's clear."

She turned to me, her gaze going to The Weeds. "Shit. That's him?"

"That's him."

I knelt by the body. His face was twisted in an expression of horror. Couldn't blame him. Besides the gaping, bloody hole in his chest, the blackened parts of his skin looked painful. He'd been tortured before death, I'd bet. His skin was cold and the blood congealed, but he didn't look like he'd been here long. I was no coroner, though, so my guess was still iffy.

"Check this out." Mari's voice made me turn. She stood in front of a table, holding up a golden medallion, her hand hovering over a box. The medallion was identical to the ones the demons had worn.

"Is that box full of those?"

"Yep. I bet it's his signature. Any demons wearing these were hired by him."

I nodded, turning back to the body. "Who the hell did you get mixed up with?"

Dead bastard said nothing.

I searched around the body, finally lifting him up to reveal a single black feather underneath. I picked it up, then turned to show Mari. "Looks like we have a clue."

Wally appeared a half second later, his keen red gaze glued

to my hand. He approached and sniffed, then drew back with a wince.

"What is it?" I asked.

That's an angel feather.

"An angel?"

Fallen angel, to be precise.

Oh shit. Was Declan the one who had killed The Weeds?

No. No way.

An hour later, we staggered out of Grimrealm. I clutched the feather as we arrived at the surface, every muscle in my body dragging with exhaustion. My veins felt like they were on fire, and it was agony.

When we arrived on our doorstep, Wally was waiting for us. He'd disappeared after identifying the feather.

The hellcat sat on the step right in front of the door, looking us up and down. *You look like hell.*

I scowled at him. "It's the curse."

You need to rest.

What I wanted to do was go hunt down Declan.

Mari touched my shoulder. "He's right. The book of curses said so."

It didn't matter whether or not I agreed—they were right. Staying rested would keep my strength up. And it was nearly four a.m.—I'd been up ages.

"Del is going to come over in the morning," Mari said. "We were going to keep working on finding whoever made the orb, but she can probably help us with the feather, too."

Having a plan made me feel better, and if we had a FireSoul on the job, our chances improved a lot.

Silently, we dragged ourselves to bed. I set the feather on the night table beside me, staring at it for just a moment.

It wasn't Declan's feather. He'd have no reason to kill The Weeds, and if he'd done it, he'd have told me.

Also, the distinctive silver tip to the feather was something I'd never seen on his wings.

Which meant there was another fallen angel out there. An immensely powerful, angry angel who'd killed my only connection to the demons who'd put the curse on me.

I'd find the bastard.

I had to.

I woke feeling a hell of a lot more human, thank fates. There was still a faint burn in my veins, but I could move more easily than I had been able to last night, when exhaustion had pulled at me like an anchor.

Mari and I met in the foyer around eight, and Del joined us a few minutes later.

"I brought presents," she said as she stepped through the front door. Her midnight hair gleamed brightly in the early morning sun, and her black leather jacket was beaten and worn. From the look of the sword slice on the right arm, it'd seen some serious action lately.

My eyes went immediately to the paper cups in her hands. They were emblazoned with the familiar logo of Potions & Pastilles.

"You are a saint." I took the coffee and sipped deeply. "I owe you one."

"Then you're about to lose your mind." She drew a paper sack from the bag at her side. "Cinnamon buns."

I took the bag. "You're welcome to visit any time."

Mari and I led her into my kitchen. We sat at the table, and I pushed the feather across the gleaming white surface toward her. "I know that you're here to help Mari find the origin of the orb, but we were hoping you could give this a look."

Mari had a bit of seeker ability, and she'd already tried to find the origin of the feather with her magic. No luck, though.

Del picked up the feather. "Tell me what you know about it."

I described the crime scene from last night, including the bit about Wally identifying the feather as belonging to a fallen angel.

When I finished, Del closed her eyes, and her magic flared. I held my breath as she worked. When her brow furrowed and lines of worry cut in around her mouth, disappointment welled.

She opened her bright blue eyes. "I'm sorry. I'm getting nothing. I think there's a protection charm on it. Something that hides the original owner from tracking charms and the like."

"I can't say that I'm surprised." Mari crossed her legs and sat back, folding her arms over her chest. Today, she was dressed in her black leather fight wear, since she was planning to get right to work with Del, tracking the orb. Her hair was done up in a high ponytail, and her usual black eye makeup obscured much of her face. "Someone that powerful—a fallen angel committing murder—will have access to good spells to cover their tracks."

Mari met my eyes, and she knew exactly what I was going to have to do now. "I'll go with Del to try to track the shards of the orb. That's as likely to lead us to the answer as the medallion. You're going to go to Declan?"

"He's the only fallen angel I know, so yes."

She nodded. "Good luck."

"Thanks." I was going to need it.

A half hour later, I found myself standing outside Declan's building in the Business District. It was one of the tallest buildings in town, and the bottom half contained offices.

The top, however, were some swanky penthouses that I'd never been inside. I looked down at the note he'd left for me a few days ago. It had his phone number and his address written at the bottom, and since he hadn't picked up the phone, here I was.

It took a little fast talking to get past the security guard, but I managed. At the top floor, I went to the apartment on the left and banged on the door.

After a few minutes, when there was no answer, I pressed my ear to the door. There was a noise coming from within. A rushing kind of sound, or a low rumble.

I pulled my lock-picking kit from my pocket and knelt down, making quick work of the lock. When I pushed open the door, I figured it out almost immediately.

Declan was in the shower.

That was probably why he hadn't answered my call.

I strolled into the massive apartment. The style was simple and modern, and I'd bet twenty bucks that he'd hired someone to fill it with furniture. He didn't seem like the type to hit up an Ikea. It was nice, though, and expensive. Clearly, bounty hunting paid well.

I strode toward the massive wall of windows that ran along two sides of the apartment, taking in the view of the city below. At night, the city lights would sparkle like stars. Right now, I had an amazing view of the ocean on the other side of town, gleaming a midnight blue beneath the sun.

The shower water turned off, and I frowned.

On one hand, I'd just broken into his apartment and was about to ask him for help. Maybe that wasn't ideal, from a manners standpoint.

On the other hand, the damage was already done.

So I took a seat on the massive gray sofa, leaning back and draping an arm over the low back.

When Declan walked out with just a white towel around his waist, I couldn't help the wolf whistle.

It was meant as a joke, but honestly, the sight of his broad chest and powerful arms did deserve a second look.

I couldn't help it, but a connection forged between us immediately. It crackled like a live wire as our eyes met.

I hadn't seen him in five days, but I hadn't forgotten this.

How could I?

There was no surprise on his face as he looked at me. "I thought I heard someone enter."

"Just thought I'd pop by for a visit." I uncrossed and recrossed my legs, my gaze roving over his chest. "Can't say I have any complaints about the welcome committee."

The corner of his mouth picked up in a smile, and I rose, unable to help myself. He called me to him like a moth to flame, and I strolled across the room toward him.

As I walked, memories of our kiss flashed in my mind. Of his lips on mine, his strong shoulders beneath my hands. It had made me lightheaded then, and it made me lightheaded now. There was no fighting it.

I stopped in front of him, looking up into his face.

"You never called me back." His voice was a low rumble.

"I'm here now, aren't I?"

He smiled fully, having a devastating effect on my composure.

"And I did call," I said to distract myself. "You just didn't pick up."

"When?"

"Twenty minutes ago."

"So you came right down here?"

"Couldn't wait." In the back of my mind, I knew there was a reason I was here. It was important—extremely important. But for this very moment, I could only see him. Smell him. The scent of a rainstorm wrapped around me, heady and fierce.

I wanted him.

More than I ever had before.

I leaned forward, pressing a hand to his arm. I leaned up to kiss him.

5

THOUGH HEAT DARKENED HIS EYES AS I APPROACHED FOR THE KISS, the muscle in his arm jumped slightly beneath my fingertips. Flinching.

Shit.

Reality crashed back into me.

The nullifying power.

I withdrew my hand, and sank back onto my heels.

He frowned, a protest in his eyes, and his big hand landed on my waist, as if he didn't want to let me step away from him.

I caught sight of a tightening around his lips, a barely perceptible sign of discomfort.

I pulled away from him. "You can feel my nullifying power."

"Not enough to bother me."

"Of course it bothers you. I can see it." And I'd heard Cass describe it once. How it felt like it was sucking out your soul.

"That's my problem, not yours," he said.

Everything that had gone unsaid after we'd last seen each other hung in the air. The memory of that kiss sparked, along with the fact that I'd finally started to trust him.

Then...nothing.

Because of the nullifying magic that I'd created to help defeat the Oraxia demon, I couldn't be with him without making him ill.

So I'd stepped back.

There was no point in pursuing something like this, and it was for the best.

Feeling was too dangerous. Trusting was too dangerous. Because I wasn't just trusting him with the secret of my true nature. If I got too close to him, I could be trusting him with my heart.

So not worth it.

I didn't want to talk about this now. I couldn't. So I reached into my pocket and pulled out the feather, then held it up in front of him.

Annoyance flashed on his face—probably because I was changing the subject—but his attention zoomed in on the feather, as I'd thought it might.

"Recognize it?" I asked.

He frowned, reaching up to take the feather from me. His hand brushed against mine—a deliberate gesture, I was sure—and I couldn't process how I felt about it.

So I focused on the problem at hand. Considering it was a problem that could kill me, it was where my attention needed to be.

"It's from a fallen." His frown deepened as he turned the feather around, inspecting it from every angle.

"Found it under the body of The Weeds."

"Dead body?" he asked.

"Yes. Dead as a doornail, with his heart ripped out. And some burn marks on his skin."

"That's interesting."

"Does it give you a hint who the feather might belong to?"

"No, but I wonder if removing the heart was a message. Or if he wanted the heart."

"The Weeds had weak magic, so I can't imagine he wanted the heart. But I've no idea."

Declan frowned. "A message, then. Not to mess with him."

"It makes sense. We think—hope—that The Weeds hooked the fallen angel up with the demons who attacked our house yesterday."

Declan's gaze sharpened on me, worry flickering in their depths. "But you're okay, right?"

Ooh, shit.

What should I tell him?

I was so used to playing it close to the vest that my first instinct was to lie and say I was fine.

But I could *die.*

I had just days to catch this fallen angel and find the cure, and I'd need all the help I could get. Dedicated help.

And didn't I owe it to Declan?

We didn't know each other well, but there had almost been something between us. Even if there couldn't be now, I didn't want to tell giant lies anymore. It was starting to weigh too heavily on me.

"It depends on how you define *okay*," I said.

"If you have to say that, then you're not okay at all." He gripped both my upper arms, concern digging deep lines into his forehead. I tried to pull back, but he didn't let me. He wouldn't let me go until I told him exactly what was going on with me. That was clear enough.

"They hit me and Mari with some kind of curse. It lights a fire in our veins that will burn until we're dead."

His skin paled and his grip tightened. "You have only days."

"You've heard of the curse?"

He nodded. "Fire veins. And you think the fallen hired the demons who did this?"

"It's one of our only clues. The demons who attacked us were wearing the same charm as the necromancer and Oraxia demon from before. They're all connected. Mari is tracking our only other clue—the fragments of one of the orbs that was used to turn Magic's Bend inhabitants to stone."

"And you want my help tracking this feather."

"Exactly. Will you?"

He gave me a look that suggested I was an idiot for even asking.

"Let me get dressed. We need to move on this right away." He withdrew his hands, and I stepped back, knowing that I was being a weirdo but unable to help it.

I waited while he dressed, inspecting his apartment. There weren't many personal touches here. He didn't live in this space —he just existed in it. I'd bet a hundred bucks he was one of those people married to his work.

But then, it was important work.

A few minutes later, he returned, dressed in dark jeans and a black, long-sleeved shirt. He gestured me forward. "Come on. We can start our search in here."

"In here?"

But he'd already disappeared through the doorway.

I followed him, the feather gripped between my fingers. The hallway led past an enormous bedroom with a sweeping view of the sea in the distance, to a room filled with so much technology that I stopped dead in my tracks, staring.

"What the hell is this?" I asked, my gaze moving over monitors and bits and bobs of metal that I didn't recognize.

"Don't really have a name for it." He turned to me, a grin stretching across his face. "How about command center?"

I approached a flat table that had crystals arranged on it. Massive amounts of magic radiated from the colorful rocks.

I pointed to it. "This must do something interesting."

Declan joined me. "This place is my side project, though it helps with the bounty hunting."

I looked up at him. "You've joined magic and technology, haven't you? And you use it to find your targets."

"That's the gist of it." He pointed to the crystal setup. "This is primarily magic. It can replicate a spell." He turned to a huge computer monitor that flashed with a dozen languages. "And that can find people based upon their known magical signature. Though it doesn't always work. Still got some kinks to work out on that one."

"You invented all this?" I asked.

"In my free time. I enjoy it."

"Wild." I held up the feather. "So, what have you got that can help us with this?"

"Probably not much, given that it's the feather of a fallen, but we can get a few clues before we go to the High Court of the Angels."

"We'd *go* there?"

He nodded. "If we want more info, yes."

Shit. "I'm not going to like, burst into flames when I arrive or anything, am I?"

I had a bit of a shady past, at least as far as a bunch of angels would be concerned.

Declan grinned. "You'll be fine. You're no worse than I am. We wouldn't be invited to stay, or given access to all of the High Court or heavenly realms, but we can at least get an audience and ask some questions."

"Well, then. Let's give it a go."

Declan held out his hand for the feather, and I gave it to him. He strode to the corner of the room where a complicated setup of coils of silver and golden wire were positioned over a steel platform. Magic sparked around the coils, feeling like tiny pinpricks of energy.

"What is this thing?" I asked as he laid the feather down on the metal platform.

"It helps determine the age of the magic in an object. All magic decays at a certain rate. A bit like the half-life on carbon. Using that theory, I built this to determine how old an object is."

"Ah, that's pretty cool." Magical decay was a big issue, especially for objects that weren't living. Eventually, an object that was enchanted with a powerful spell would decay to the point where it would explode.

I watched Declan fiddle with some dials. It was rare to see technology and magic combined in such a way. Often, they weren't very compatible. "So, you're some kind of genius, huh?"

He shrugged. "Not sure genius is the word. I just like to fiddle with things."

"This is a long way from the demon battlefields." The story he'd told me of fighting on the front lines of the angel-demon wars was still stuck in my head.

"Can't say I mind," he said. "I enjoyed aspects of military life, but watching your friends die sucks."

I nodded. I'd been lucky in my life. I'd never had many friends, and those I did have were immensely powerful. Their magic protected them—made them great fighters—so the worst I'd had to see were a lot of grievous injuries.

But I imagined that what he'd experienced wasn't too far off of the fear I'd felt as a child when Aunt and Uncle had threatened Mari with bodily harm if I didn't comply with their demands. Especially given the fact that they'd often followed through on their threats.

Magic sparked more fiercely around the metal coils, and the feather began to vibrate. Pale green light glowed from the contraption, and a tiny computer screen began to blink with some words.

"What language is that in?" I asked.

"High Angelic."

"I didn't realize you had a language."

"We do, though we keep it quiet. That way, no one outside of our ranks can interpret any lost communication. It worked well during the demon wars."

"Well, what does it say?" I squinted at the weird writing that flowed by on the screen.

Declan finished reading, then turned to me. "Older than written record, but the feather has only been off the angel for two days."

"So The Weeds was killed two days ago."

"I'd be comfortable assuming that."

This angel had a two-day lead on us. Dang it.

"One more test." Declan picked up the feather and went to the other side of the room, where a vat of sparkling viscous goo sat under a gleaming pink light. "This will determine what kind of magical powers the angel has. Hopefully."

He dunked the feather in the goo, then fiddled with some dials. A moment later, magic sparked on the air, sharp and stinging. I flinched.

Declan stuck his hand into the goo, then winced.

"What is it?"

"Feels like the angel can emit electrical shocks if you touch him."

"Like lightning?"

"Roughly, yes."

"And this contraption works by hitting you with the magic that the object possesses?"

"A more minor version of it, yes."

"That makes sense, given the burns I saw on The Weeds." I

studied Declan's pale face as he drew the feather out of the sparkling goo.

"We won't want to let him lay his hands on us, that's for sure." He looked around the room, then nodded his head slightly, as if he'd made up his mind. "That's about all we can do here. We can go to the High Court if you're ready."

"You have time? You can just drop whatever you're working on?"

He gave me a long look. "You're cursed with deadly fire. I think I can clear my schedule to help you fix that."

"And by 'fix that,' you mean *not die*."

"Yep. And we should get a move on."

I saluted him. "Agreed." Then I lowered my hand, feeling a bit awkward. "And thanks. For helping me."

He nodded.

I didn't know where we stood now, but I appreciated him. A lot.

"Come on. We need to head to the roof."

"The roof?"

"Only one way to get to heaven." He shot me a grin. "Not that it's actually heaven. More like angel headquarters."

"Then let's go." I followed him out of the apartment to a stairwell that led to the roof.

We climbed quickly, reaching the top a few moments later. There was a pavilion with chairs and a grill, along with a few trees in massive pots.

Wind tore at my hair, and I sucked in the fresh air. It was so mundane compared to the laboratory down below. But nice. "Not a bad place to spend time."

"Theoretically, I agree. Haven't had time, though."

"Too busy hunting demons?"

"Exactly." He gestured me toward him. "No way to do this without me holding on to you."

I hesitated, keenly aware of what touching me meant.

"I'm not as worried about it as you are," he said, clearly reading my mind.

"Well, you should be."

"I'm not." He gently grabbed my arm and yanked me to him.

I gasped, clutching his shoulders as heat flared within me. "Well, all right, then."

He nodded, satisfied. "Hang on tight."

I wrapped my arms around his neck, searching his face for any sign of discomfort. There might have been a slight tightening of his lips, but it was hard to say, exactly.

When his strong arms went under my legs and he hoisted me up into the air, I gasped. He held me tight to him, his warm body heating my own, and my head nearly spun.

Damn, I wanted him.

His massive wings shot out from his back, a midnight display that took my breath away.

He launched us into the air, and I looked down, watching Magic's Bend recede into the distance.

"So we just...go up until we hit it?" I asked, the breeze tearing at my hair.

"Pretty much. There is a portal in the sky that can only be accessed by angels and their passengers."

I wrapped my arms more tightly around his neck, partially for safety and partially for my own satisfaction. I couldn't help the images that flashed through my mind as we headed upward —memories of us kissing, of us rolling around on the boat in the Bermuda Triangle.

"Doesn't touching me bother you?" I asked. "I can feel my nullifying power affecting you."

"It's fine."

"Fine? Feeling like your magic—and your soul—is being sucked out is fine?"

"It's not a problem."

His face looked really strained though. "It's making it harder for you to fly, isn't it? Your magic is repressed."

"It's a little more difficult, but it's not a problem."

Yeah, we definitely weren't flying as fast as we normally would. My magic was repressing his. "You're just ignoring it."

"I create my own reality." His smiled. "And frankly, touching you is worth it."

I doubted that.

"There's ways around everything," he said. "I can get used to it. Or we can try to fix it."

"Fix it? How?"

"I don't know. But we're smart. If we put our heads together, we can figure something out."

I didn't think it was possible to get rid of magic once I had it. And anyway, maybe it was a sign. I'd started to trust him, but that was a bad idea. Being alone had worked for a long time. I hardly knew him, and perhaps this was a signal from the universe that I should focus on other things in my life. Namely, staying alive. Doing my work for the Council of Demon Slayers.

Declan looked like he was about to say something, but I felt a surge of magic from behind.

His gaze moved to the spot off my left shoulder. "We're here. Hold on tight."

I gripped him closely, pressing myself against him. "Ready."

He flew toward the magic, which grew stronger with every meter traveled. A faint golden light grew brighter as we approached, until finally, the ether sucked me in and spun me around.

Declan's grip tightened, as if he didn't want to lose me in the maelstrom.

Finally, the ether spit us out in the middle of a pale blue sky. Fluffy clouds surrounded us, and I leaned over to peer down. A vast white city stretched below us. Buildings from every period in history appeared to coexist side by side, each situated along a wide lane. There were no cars, and no people that I could see, but the place thrummed with energy.

"This is where the angels live?" I looked at Declan. "Where are they?"

"There aren't as many as there used to be." He lowered us to the ground. "Many leave, like I did."

We landed in the middle of a courtyard. A massive fountain bubbled away to our left. The sky overhead was a deep, bright blue.

I let go of Declan, stepping aside almost reluctantly. "Which way do we go?"

"To the High Court. Come on." He led the way down the wide lanes toward a massive biding with huge white columns. Powerful magic emanated from the structures, making my muscles quiver.

Declan strode up the massive front steps as if he owned the place.

I hurried to join him. "So, what's the relationship between angels and fallen angels like?"

"Generally, it's tense." He shrugged. "Angels don't understand why some choose to fall. We don't understand why they stayed. Especially after the demon wars ended. But ours is a good relationship, otherwise. In some cases, it can be downright violent. Everyone falls differently. Our feather owner, for instance, probably isn't allowed to visit here. He's made his stance quite clear with the heart ripping."

"Yes, I imagine the angels don't agree with murder."

"You'd be surprised. But they generally only want it to happen on their terms."

Angels approving of murder? Fighting the demon wars was one thing. This was another thing entirely. Life was never what you expected, though, and angels were apparently no different.

At the top of the sweeping steps, massive golden doors rose tall and broad. Declan swung one open, and we entered a huge hall with a soaring ceiling.

I looked up toward a mosaic of glass tiles that appeared to depict brilliant clouds and a blazing sun. When I looked back down, Wally had appeared next to me. The little black cat's back was arched, and his smoky fur wafted wildly.

He hissed, bright red eyes flashing to mine. *You're on angel turf?*

"Not expecting that?"

No. See you later. He disappeared, clearly irritated and freaked out.

"Seems your hellcat isn't a fan of angels."

"I suppose it makes sense." I turned in a circle, taking in the many huge doors that led off of the entryway. "Which one?"

Declan pointed to one that was at my left, then headed toward it. "This one, most likely. It leads to the meeting chambers, and you can almost always guarantee that you'll find some of the High Court there."

We strode toward it, our footsteps silent on the marble floor. Declan pulled open the door and stepped through. I followed, muscles tense. Angels were majorly powerful, and we were sneaking up on them. I trusted Declan to not lead us into trouble, but I couldn't fight my natural wariness. When I didn't know exactly what I was walking into, my subconscious always filled in the blanks with *death.*

6

I STEPPED INTO THE HUGE, DARKLY PANELED ROOM, MY GAZE GOING immediately to the five figures seated at a massive round table. Their combined magical signatures nearly bowled me over. I felt like I'd been hit in the face.

The sound of clashing swords and the terror of war emitted from the angel on the far right. She was tall with broad shoulders and a slicing scar across her face that had to have been delivered by a sword. A battle angel, no doubt.

The angel on the far left had a magical signature that felt like the pages of a book beneath my fingertips. It sounded like the scratch of a pen against paper. He was a slight man, with pale eyes and a thin mouth.

The three angels in the middle had signatures that I didn't even understand. One of the women had a power that felt like judgment, which was nearly impossible to describe but extremely distinct. Another's felt like drowning. That particular angel looked cruel, with dark eyes and a severe face atop a skinny body.

Mental note—stay the hell away from that dude.

The last angel sat with a serene look on her face, her eyes nearly closed, and she murmured something under her breath. She looked as old as time itself. She was in a trance of some kind, and I consciously lightened my footsteps even more, despite the fact that they were silent.

"High Court." Declan's strong voice filled the space.

The five figures stood, even the one who had been in a trance. Surprise flashed across some faces, irritation across others. But all of them bowed low.

I looked at Declan, impressed.

He inclined his head.

Ooh boy.

That was clear enough. Declan might be the fallen angel and these guys might be the official ones, but it was clear that the five of them really respected him. They held their bows for a moment longer, then rose.

"Declan O'Shea." The battle angel stepped forward, her simple leather clothes a contrast to the ornate robes worn by the other angels. "We're honored by your presence. But this is a rare occasion. What brings you to us?"

"We are here tracking a fallen." He gestured to me. "Aerdeca is from Magic's Bend, and she found an angel's feather beneath the body of a murdered Magica called The Weeds."

The five angels frowned.

"That's odd," said the scholarly angel with the pale eyes. "May we see this feather?"

Declan pulled it from his pocket and handed it over.

The man took it and studied it, a crease at his brow. "The white tip is unusual."

I held my breath as the angels passed it around. Surely one of them would recognize it. There was confusion on most faces, until the feather reached the hands of the oldest angel—the woman who had been in the trance.

She gripped the feather and raised it to her face, squinting at it. She gasped. "Acius."

The other angels turned to her.

"Acius?" The battle angel's voice sounded skeptical. "He's a myth."

The oldest angel shook her head slowly. "The white tips on the end. Only one angel has ever had that, and we haven't seen him in centuries. Millennia."

"Is he a fallen?" Declan asked.

The old angel's eyes flicked to him. "Most certainly."

"What did he do to fall?" I asked.

The other angels moved closer to the oldest one. Closing ranks.

She snapped her mouth shut.

The battle angel looked from Declan to me. "This is a matter for the High Court."

The other angels nodded.

"We will take care of it," said the scholarly angel. "Thank you for bringing it to our attention."

Whoa.

That was a clear dismissal.

I looked at Declan. A frown stretched across his face. The air in the room became prickly. Some kind of charm was igniting—one to make it clear that we were no longer welcome.

What the heck were we supposed to do now? We couldn't start a fight in the High Court. I looked to Declan for guidance. Normally, I liked to lead the charge. But I was *way* out of my depth here.

Declan nodded. "Thank you."

He turned to leave without another word, so I followed. We strode quickly from the room. As we neared the door, it opened for us.

"They're ready to get rid of us," I murmured.

"Indeed, they are."

When we reached the far side of the entry foyer, those doors opened as well. They were *really* ready to get rid of us. Despite the great respect they'd shown for Declan, this was something that freaked them out so much they'd shut him out.

As soon as we exited and reached the open courtyard, I turned to Declan. "What the hell was that all about?"

"They're closing ranks. They don't want anyone to know what Acius has done. Or what he is. It's a mess, clearly. Something they want to clean up on their own."

"That's stupid. We can help."

He nodded. "That's the High Court for you, though."

"No wonder you chose to fall. The bureaucracy seems like a nightmare."

"It is." He gestured to the silent city around us. "Not to mention this place. Perfect and perfectly ordered...an extension of the strict hierarchy that keeps the High Court in the past."

"It slows them down if they won't accept outside help. How is this any different than your bounty-hunting jobs for them?"

"This is a fallen angel. A dangerous one, from the sounds of it. They'll want to handle it themselves."

"You're sure they're not on his side?" Even as I said it, I knew how unlikely it was.

"No, they're not. If they were, they'd fall without choosing to do so and be magically evicted from the High Court. The mere fact that they are still in that building makes it clear they are on the side of right."

"But they won't catch him. Not quickly, at least."

"Most likely, yes. But at least we have a clue. The name Acius."

"How do we track that?"

"The Heavenly Archives. When I fell, I lost my access, but we can break in."

I raised my brows. "Ooh, break in? Not very angelic of you."

He just grinned. "That's why I'm a fallen. Now come on. We've got some B&E to do."

Declan led me through the courtyard and down a wide avenue lined with white stone buildings. The whole area was as quiet as a tomb.

"Wow, a lot of angels really have left, huh?"

He nodded. "Most were killed in the demon wars. Many who weren't, left. This life is too different from that one. Once you're used to the battlefield, you don't want to come back here."

I couldn't blame them. This was just too perfect. Wally had definitely wanted to have nothing to do with it.

"We're nearly there." Declan pointed ahead, to a spot where it seemed like the world ended. The road disappeared into nothingness, giving way to the vastness of blue sky.

"What the hell?"

"Angelic headquarters are built on an island in the sky."

I stepped up to the edge of the road and looked down into nothingness. Clouds floated below. "Holy fates, so this is why humans think angels live on clouds."

"They aren't far off." He pointed to the right, and I leaned around to look across the edge of the floating island.

A long, narrow bridge stretched across the open air. At the other end, it connected to a towering building that gleamed golden and white. The building itself looked like a mountain, with turrets and towers piercing the clouds.

"That's the Heavenly Archives?" It was *big*.

"It is. Thousands of years old, with records of almost anything you can think of."

"So we'll just fly over?" That bridge looked skinny and rickety, the way it dangled over open nothingness.

"Unfortunately, no. There's a spell that prevents flying, since that's the way most angels would choose to break in."

"Ah, shit." I eyed the bridge warily. "So we're taking that thing, then?"

"That's the plan. Come on."

We walked along the edge of the floating island. Clouds drifted past, reminding me just how high up we were. And just how far we would fall if this plan went tits up.

We reached the edge of the bridge, which looked like it was a million miles long.

"What's our plan?" I asked.

"Teamwork." He met my gaze. "Remember that trick you pulled with my memory? Think you can do that with a guard?"

"Definitely."

"That's the plan, then. A guard should meet us at the halfway point on the bridge. If we fail to convince him we should pass, we'll fall."

I looked down, then said dryly, "I'll endeavor to be convincing."

"You can do it."

"I'm going to become invisible so I can sneak up on him while you distract him." I stepped onto the bridge, my breath held. I'd never really been afraid of heights, but this was another thing altogether.

Declan followed close behind. It was a narrow passage, meant for one, and I gripped the golden chains that acted as railings. The bridge swayed beneath my feet, and my stomach clenched.

Every step rocked the little bridge, and it took far too long to reach the middle. We were partway there when I spotted the tall figure approaching us. He was so pale he was nearly transparent, but he gleamed a perfect pearly white when the sun hit him just right.

"He's not human, is he?" I whispered back to Declan.

"No, he's a Celestial."

I'd never tried my convincing magic on a Celestial before. As he neared us, I sensed his power in a way that vibrated my bones. I'd never felt magic like that, and I had no idea what he could do.

"Greetings, Pelatin!" Declan shouted from behind me.

Pelatin had very indistinct features—a narrow nose, small lips, and pale eyes. A bit like the popular conception of an alien. It was hard to read his expression, but he had an air of suspicion about him.

When he spoke, his voice confirmed it. "I thought you fell, Declan."

"A bit of a misunderstanding," Declan said.

I was only about ten feet from Pelatin now. I tried to match my stride to Declan's so my footsteps didn't rock the bridge at all. Hopefully Pelatin wouldn't sense my magic. I drew in a deep breath, trying to gather my signature to me. The nullifying magic was the hardest bit—that was new and difficult to control.

"You know that fallen are not permitted to access the Heavenly Archives." Pelatin's voice rang with authority. He clearly did not believe Declan's story about a misunderstanding.

But I was nearly to him. I just had to get up close and touch him. I hurried my steps, staying as silent as I could as I sliced my thumbnail against my finger. Pain spiked, then white blood welled. As soon as I stood in front of him, I reached up and swiped my fingertip across his forehead.

He flinched when he felt my featherlight touch.

"Let us pass," I whispered, imbuing my words with my suggestive magic. "We should be here. We have access."

He blinked, clearly confused.

"Let us pass," I repeated the words. "We should be here."

Finally, he nodded, then gestured toward the Heavenly Archives behind him.

"Of course, Declan. You are welcome here."

I glanced back at Declan, whose lips were quirked up in a small smile. "Thank you, Pelatin."

Pelatin inclined his head, then turned and started up the bridge. He moved quickly, and I hurried to keep up, still stuck between him and Declan. I kept my hood up, careful to make sure the wind didn't blow it over.

As we neared the other side, the walls rose tall in front of us. They were massive, made of white stone shot through with gold. I followed Pelatin through the arch and into a small courtyard. Three streets diverged off the courtyard, all of which were surrounded by huge buildings. There was the sense that the buildings continued for miles.

This place was so big it almost defied the imagination.

Once on solid ground, Pelatin turned left and disappeared into a small guardhouse.

Declan joined me and leaned close, whispering, "Just walk forward. Follow me."

I touched his arm lightly to indicate that I understood, and he set off down the main road that was right in front of us. He waved goodbye to Pelatin as he passed.

Once we were out of earshot, I leaned close. "Now what?"

"Now we scale the wall of the main building."

"Ooh, a true B&E?" I asked.

"I think it's the best way. Pelatin is just the bridge guard. There are more at the main entrance. Too many to persuade all at once. And I don't want to fight the angels."

I could see how fighting his former comrades would sit wrong.

"This way." Declan turned right down a narrow side street.

Buildings towered on either side of us, each wall dotted with tiny windows. They were unusually small, probably to protect the books and documents within from sun damage.

"This place is quiet," I murmured. "Where is everyone?"

"Guards and scholars are inside with the texts. Every building is full of books and records. No one lives here, so it's not like a normal city."

My shoulders relaxed slightly at the idea that we probably wouldn't run into anyone.

Declan led us in a loop back toward the edge of the floating island. Just like at the main angel headquarters, the street disappeared into nothingness at the edge. In some places, tall walls extended up from the edge, the libraries built up right next to nothingness.

I looked at Declan. "You have got to be kidding me. You want us to climb up a wall that is right over open space, don't you?"

He looked toward my voice, though his eyes didn't land right on me since I was still invisible. "Yeah, pretty much. The protection charms are weakest at the edges here, since most wouldn't be brave enough to climb up a wall like this."

"Dumb enough is more like."

He grinned. "Dumb enough. Come on. You ready?"

"Yeah." What was my alternative, anyway? Even now, I could feel the fire in my veins. It grew with every hour, and eventually it would consume me from within. Might as well risk my life to avoid that horrible death.

Declan moved to the edge of the buildings, and I joined him, careful not to look at the clouds below. The side of the building was almost too smooth for climbing, but there were a few handholds where the great stone blocks met each other.

Declan began to scale his way upward. I flipped my hood back so I became visible. Somehow, it seemed even worse to fall off and plummet to my death without anyone ever seeing it happen.

Shut up, self.

Dumb, dangerous thoughts.

I climbed onto the building, following carefully in Declan's wake. My heart thundered and my skin chilled as the wind tore at my hair. Declan took a circuitous route to the top, but it had the best handholds. My fingertips hurt from clinging to the tiny bits of stone, but I held on for dear life.

"Almost there," Declan murmured.

I drew in a deep breath and continued climbing, every atom of my body totally alive and terrified as I ascended. Finally, I gripped the top of the building.

Declan's hand closed around my wrist, and he pulled me up the last little bit. I scrambled onto the small deck, gasping.

"Thank fates that's over." I turned to take in the view.

More clouds.

So many clouds.

I hated clouds.

I turned back to Declan, then eyed the small patio upon which we stood. There was a little door. "Is that our way in?"

"It is. We just need to break it down."

My brows shot upward. "Break it down? Won't people hear us do that?"

"There's a chance, but hopefully not. We're at a remote part of the archives."

"Why don't we pick the locks?" I approached and knelt in front of the metal lock, inspecting it for any clue about its operation. All locks were different, and I quite enjoyed the challenge they presented.

"There's a charm that will melt the tools you use."

I grinned. I might have to live with this damned nullifying magic, but it could come in handy sometimes. "I've got just the cure for that."

Understanding dawned on his face. "Ah, of course you do."

I drew a small set of lock-picking tools from my pocket, then sorted out the tiny metal implements that I thought might work best with this particular lock.

Once I was situated, I raised my left hand to the door and pressed it to the wood. A burning sensation flared against my skin, and I winced, feeding my nullification magic into the wood as quickly as I could.

It came slowly at first, with my mind distracted by the pain, but eventually I dredged it up from my soul and forced it into the door.

The burning sensation faded, and I stuck the tiny pick into the lock. As I worked, I made sure to keep up with the nullification magic that prevented the lock from melting my tools.

"Where did you learn to do this?" Declan asked.

"When I was a kid in Grimrealm, I found a hairpin. I thought I could use it to get us out of the room my aunt sometimes locked us in. It didn't work. So I found a skinny nail. That didn't work either. But I just kept trying. Different tools—mostly trash—until finally I figured out a way."

There was silence for a moment, and I realized how shitty that sounded.

Whatever.

In hindsight, maybe I shouldn't have shared that. But whatever. My life had been shitty once. No need to hide it.

Declan's hand landed on my shoulder, a gentle touch that was obviously meant to be comforting.

Instead, it lit a small fire inside me.

I drew in a steady breath and ignored it, focusing instead on the lock in front of me.

Finally, the lock clicked, and I stood, pushing open the door.

"Nicely done." Declan sounded impressed.

I inclined my head, then stepped through the door and into a darkened room.

A black shadow rushed toward me, partly ephemeral and partly solid. White fangs and claws gleamed in the light.

A shadow wolf.

A scream trapped in my throat, and I dodged right, trying to avoid the wolf's fangs. Fear snared me as I felt the icy grip of death.

7

From behind, Declan charged the wolf.

A glint of steel flashed in the low light. He'd drawn his sword from the ether. The wolf growled, white magic spurting from its mouth. The figure was hazy.

The creature was made of angelic magic, not flesh and bone. I wouldn't have to feel guilty for killing it, since I wouldn't be so much killing as destroying the spell.

Declan lunged for the wolf with his sword.

Another appeared in the middle of the room. It crouched low, growling, its onyx eyes on me. The beast was huge, four feet tall at least.

I drew my mace from the ether, ignoring the ice that shivered over my spine. The metal of my mace chain was comforting in my hands as I began to swing.

By the time the wolf leapt for me, I had enough speed going. I slammed the mace into the wolf's head as he lunged for my face. My heart lodged in my throat.

The mace connected solidly, and the wolf disappeared with a poof of magic that smelled like rotten meat. I spun in time to see Declan plunge his blade into the other shadow wolf's chest.

The creature hissed and stumbled backward, disappearing on a poof of smoke.

Panting, I leaned against the wall. "Quite the welcoming committee."

"They sensed when we broke through the door. We shouldn't see any more."

"Unless we have to break through more doors."

Declan shrugged. "Hopefully we won't have to."

I stashed my mace in the ether, trying to calm my breathing. "Now what?"

"Let's head to the main archives. They're in this building."

He led me out of the room and into a narrow corridor. It was barely wide enough for me to slip through. Declan's shoulders brushed the edges.

"For such a big building, I expected the hallways to be wider."

"Every inch is dedicated to the archives. If it can't hold a document, it's considered unimportant. I'm amazed this place still has passageways to let people in."

Declan led me through an endless maze. At times, we passed by blank walls. Then by shelves crammed full of books. Then scrolls, paintings, stone tablets. There was no end to the information stored within this massive space. My head was spinning ten minutes later.

"How will we ever find what we're looking for?" I asked.

"Declan?" A masculine voice sounded from in front of Declan, cutting off his answer.

Immediately, I stiffened, drawing a sword from the ether. These quarters were far too close for a mace.

I tried to peer around Declan to get a look at whoever was speaking, but his broad shoulders filled the space. I ducked low and peered around his side.

An angel in simple white clothes stared at Declan, shock on his face.

"Camius," Declan said. "It's been a long time."

"Too long." Camius looked down and spotted me peering at him.

Shit.

I was basically crouched low and peeking out at him like a weirdo.

Ah well. Not my usual first impression, but you can't have everything.

"Who is your guest?" Camius asked.

I straightened. Declan turned to the side and gestured to me. I hid my sword behind my back, only increasing my awkward introduction. But it seemed we weren't going to fight, and there was no need to freak the guy out.

Declan gestured to me. "This is my, ah…friend. Aerdeca."

My ah…friend?

Okay, then. It was a loaded sentence, but it was the only way to describe what I was.

"Good to meet you." I looked between him and Declan. "What's going on here?"

"That's what I was hoping to find out," Camius said. "Last I heard, you'd fallen, Declan."

"I did. But we need information to save Aerdeca's life."

I noticed he didn't call me Aeri in public, and I appreciated it. I'd recently told him the name, but hadn't gone into detail about the fact that it was a secret.

Camius frowned. "Only angels can access the heavenly archives."

"And you're an angel."

Suddenly, I understood Declan's plan. He'd *hoped* to run into an old friend here. Because clearly, up until this point, we'd had no idea where we were going within the building, and it was big enough that we could starve to death before we found what we were looking for.

Camius sighed. "I supposed you want me to help you?"

"I'll die otherwise," I said. "And the one responsible is a fallen angel. So it's your business, too, in a sense."

Camius's gaze sharpened on mine. "Another fallen?"

"And not one as even-tempered and law-abiding as Declan." I patted his shoulder as if to make it very apparent that Declan was a good guy and Camius should want to help him. Want to help *me*.

Camius looked at Declan. "After what you did for me on the battlefield, I will help you. But we have to make it quick. I can't be spotted with you."

What had Declan done?

"Thank you." Declan's voice was heavy with gratitude.

I blinked, my eyes a bit warm.

He was only doing this for me.

Sure, he was curious about the other fallen angel. It was relevant to him. But it wasn't one of his jobs. In fact, the High Court had made it clear that we *shouldn't* pursue this.

So it was all for me.

I swallowed hard.

"What do you know about this angel?" Camius asked.

I let Declan fill him in with everything we knew.

When he finished, Camius nodded and turned. "Come this way. I know where we can look."

We followed him through a labyrinth of halls and finally stopped in a crowded alcove. The three of us barely fit as he searched through the old leather documents.

"Camius has worked here on and off for centuries," Declan murmured. "He knows where everything is."

Good thing we ran into him, then, because no way in hell we'd have found anything otherwise.

Camius sorted through a variety of books, eventually pulling out a heavy old leather one. He flipped through the pages, landing on one that looked to be smudged with ink.

My stomach pitched at the sight.

"Shit." Declan's low curse filled the space.

Camius stared at it for a long time, clearly frozen in shock. "This has never happened before." He turned to look at us, face white and eyes stark. "A book has been defaced."

"Is there any information left?" I asked, leaning close to see.

"I can perhaps make out his name. Acius. But that is all. The rest has been blacked out."

Declan reached for the book and took it.

I looked over his arm at it, frowning. Finally, I got a good look, but it was just as Camius had said. Black ink was smeared over the words.

"Whoever blacked that page out was in a hurry. They didn't even get the whole thing. They left his name." I could imagine it now, the person—Acius probably—about to be discovered by the guards. He'd splashed the ink and run.

"We can work with this," Declan said. "Is there any other place there might be information?"

"I'm afraid not," Camius said. "This is all there is about Acius. He's ancient. Far older than any other angel."

I was about to ask how old the angels were when an alarm went off. It blared loudly through the space, pounding at my ears. I slapped my hands to the sides of my head, trying to muffle the sound.

"What the hell is that?" I shouted.

"You," Camius said. "They've figured out there are intruders."

Shit.

"We need to get out of here," Declan said. "If they catch us, they'll lock us up. You'll die in captivity."

Oh fates, he was right. If there was any kind of delay in my release, the curse would get me.

I looked at Camius. "What's the fastest way out of here?"

"The only way is over the bridge."

Shit. I looked at Declan, who nodded. "He's right. We need to move. Now."

Declan tore the page out of the book, and Camius gasped.

Even Acius hadn't torn the page free. The worst of the worst, and Declan had topped it.

For me.

"Sorry about that, old friend." Declan smiled apologetically.

We turned and ran, sprinting away from the angel who stared after us in horror. I let Declan take the lead, since he theoretically knew where we were headed.

"I hope you know your way out of here." I jumped over a pile of books that sat in the middle of the narrow corridor.

"I've got a good idea." He sprinted faster, and I pushed myself to keep up.

We wound our way through the labyrinth of bookshelves and corridors, retracing the steps that Camius had taken when he'd led us to the shelf. We deviated from the path at one point, entering a stone-walled hallway that was devoid of books. It was narrow, and dark.

Growls sounded from behind me, and I nearly jumped out of my skin.

I looked behind, the hair raising on the back of my neck, and spotted three shadow wolves. They were even bigger than the ones before.

"Wolves!" I shouted.

"Trade me." Declan turned and darted behind me, throwing a blast of heavenly fire at one of the wolves. It smashed into the creature's chest, and the angelic magic apparition exploded in a poof of dust.

Declan clearly had this under control. I turned and sprinted ahead, glancing back occasionally to see Declan hurl another blast of heavenly fire at the wolves.

The alarm continued to blare, beating at my eardrums. I approached a split in the path.

"Left or right?" I shouted.

"Left!"

I veered left, looking back in time to see Declan blast the last wolf.

"Nice work." I slowed to let Declan take the lead again.

He sprinted ahead, leading us through the complicated maze of the enormous building. We entered another narrow corridor formed of piles of books and scrolls. They soared so high I almost couldn't see the tops of the shelves.

Magic prickled against my skin, the only warning that I got.

Books began to tumble off the shelves, crashing to the ground in front of us. One hit my shoulder, and pain flared.

Damn, they're heavy.

I drew my shield from the ether and raised it over my head. Declan did the same. I sprinted forward, leaping over fallen books. Every time one of them hit my shield, my arms vibrated from the blow. It hurt like hell after a while, my arms weakening despite my unusual strength.

More fell, faster and faster. If we didn't get out of here—or stop them—enough could fall that they would bury us.

Then the angels would come.

An idea came to mind. I stuck my hand out, running it across the shelves to the left as the books continued to fall. I could feel the magic in the shelves. It was a protective charm that turned the books into weapons.

I called upon the nullifying magic deep in my soul. It surged to life, always waiting close to the surface. I pushed it into the shelves, envisioning the protective spell failing and the books staying safely on their shelves.

Magic sparked along my arm, feeding into the wooden shelves. The books slowed, fewer and fewer falling, until they stopped.

"Is that you?" Declan shouted.

"Yeah." I kept up the magic, clearing the path as we sprinted. "You can stash your shield."

We both put our shields back in the ether and kept running. My lungs heaved and my muscles burned, but we managed to leave the books behind. Declan led us through a small room and a huge door. We spilled out into a massive entryway. It was the size and shape of a football field, with a golden ceiling soaring high above.

"Holy fates." Awe surged through me.

This place was magnificent.

"The only room not full of books," Declan said.

I sprinted up beside him to join him now that the corridor wasn't so narrow. We ran down the middle of the enormous entryway. Either side of us was bordered by stone statues of angels. As we crossed the middle of the room, magic sparked on the air.

The statue to my left leapt off the pedestal, then his stone feet hit the marble floor with a thud. He was at least six feet tall, an angel with his wings flared and a sword gripped in his hand.

Oh, fates.

Another statue burst to life at Declan's side. He turned to charge toward it.

I drew my mace from the ether and charged. The weight was heavy and comforting in my hand as I swung the weapon. The angel raised his sword as I neared, but he never got a chance to deliver a blow. I smashed my mace against his stone skull.

His head shattered, and shards of rock went flying. I darted left to avoid them, then sprinted toward the exit. To my left, Declan slammed his blade against his statue's neck. He struck with such force that the neck broke and the head tumbled off.

Next to me, Wally appeared out of thin air. The tiny black cat sprinted forward, smoky fur wafting in the wind.

"I thought you hated this place?" My words escaped through gasps.

You're about to need my help.

The cat had no sooner spoken than six more statues burst to life all at once. Some had wings, some didn't. All carried weapons as they charged.

"Ah, shit. Good timing, Wally."

Anytime. He charged the nearest statue, leapt into the air, and slammed his four feet against the statue's chest with such force that the stone man flew backward and crashed into the ground.

I left Wally to it and charged the statue to my right. I got a good swing going on the mace and banged it against the statue's head. Stone burst apart, a shard slicing against my cheek.

Pain shot through me, but I ignored it, turning to face a second statue. It had the jump on me, and was already so close that I had to duck low to avoid the sweep of the statue's blade. Stone swords couldn't cut me, but they could probably shatter bone. Or my skull.

The stone sword whizzed overhead, and I lunged to the right, buying myself some space. I swung my mace, aiming for the statue's middle. I hit him with such force that my mace crashed right through. The top half of the statue toppled to the ground, shattering.

On the other side of the room, Declan beheaded two of the figures in quick succession, while Wally smashed another to the ground.

I sprinted for the door at the far end of the hall. With every step I took, another statue came to life. There were too many to fight, though. Eventually they'd overwhelm us all.

Fighting was all well and good, but right now, we needed speed. I stashed my mace in the ether and sprinted.

"Come on, guys!" I shouted.

Declan left the fight behind, but Wally seemed to be having too much fun, slamming into statue after statue like a tiny rocket. He had the magic to get himself out of there whenever he felt like it, so I left him to it. And anyway, he was helping to clear a path for us.

Together, Declan and I sprinted out of the main doors and into the courtyard. I recognized it from earlier. We were close to the bridge. It was right ahead.

I picked up speed, pushing my aching lungs and muscles to the limit. The sun shone overhead, fierce and bright. When Pelatin appeared in front of us, blocking the bridge, I almost missed him.

"I'll leave this one up to you," I said between pants. I could smash my mace into Pelatin to get him to move, but I didn't want to hurt a real angel. Not when he was Declan's buddy and was just doing his job.

Declan raised a hand that glowed with heavenly fire.

I gasped, horrified.

He hurled the blast at Pelatin. It slammed right into the angel's chest, and the man smashed backward onto the ground, unconscious.

"It doesn't kill him," Declan said, as if reading my mind. "Heavenly fire can't really hurt angels. Worst it can do is knock us unconscious."

Thank fates. I had a feeling Declan would have regretted killing Pelatin. And since we were here to save me and Mari from a curse, I couldn't have lived with myself.

We approached Pelatin, who lay stone cold on the ground in

front of the bridge, and dodged around his form. Declan led the way onto the bridge, and my heart leapt into my throat as I took the first step onto the swinging surface.

Below me, clouds drifted by.

Oh fates, oh fates, oh fates.

Declan sprinted onto the bridge, and I followed, gripping the golden rope railings as the bridge pitched back and forth with every footfall. The wind tore at my hair, and I felt like I was a floating in the middle of the sky, about to plummet to my death at any moment. From behind, the alarm continued to blare. More angels would be coming, no doubt.

Magic wrapped around me, binding my power. It almost felt stronger than before, as if the bridge had realized that we were intruders and was determined to repress our magic so we couldn't do anything funny.

We were to the middle of the bridge when I spotted the forces on the other side. Angels mounted on horses. Battle angels, from the looks of them. Their golden armor glinted in the sun, and each held a sword as long as my leg. None of them took to the air, and surprise flashed through me.

Oh, right.

It was impossible to fly in the space between the main headquarters and the Heavenly Archives.

"Should we go back?" I shouted.

"Nope." He sounded so certain that I looked back to see why.

Another group of angels stood at that side of the bridge. There were actually even more.

Holy fates.

Even Wally couldn't get us out of this one.

When the bridge disappeared from under me, I was too shocked to even scream. Wind blasted me as I fell, and my stomach leapt into my throat. Declan plummeted in front of me.

Holy fates, we are going to die.

8

PANIC WAS A LIVING, CLAWING THING INSIDE ME AS I FELL THROUGH the wide-open sky, thousands of feet above the earth. I could feel the binding spell still wrapped around my power, keeping it repressed inside my chest. Not that I had any magic that could help in a situation like this.

Declan did, but his wings remained trapped.

Clouds whipped past us as we fell, and we plummeted through thick banks of mist. Fear like I'd never known filled me, dread nearly suffocating any instincts I had.

Think, damn it. Think.

I was so close to Declan that I could almost touch him. I wanted to, if only for comfort.

No.

No giving up yet.

I could no longer see the islands of the angelic headquarters above us, but their magic still bound my own.

An idea flared.

"Declan!" I screamed. "Reach back!"

He couldn't turn in midair, but he managed to reach his hand back. I reached my own forward, desperate to grab onto him. My idea might be impossible, but I had to try. Fear tingled across every inch of my skin as I stretched for him.

Finally, my fingertips touched his. I stretched a tiny bit farther, every muscle in my arm burning, until I grabbed his hand. We yanked ourselves toward each other, then grabbed on. I wrapped myself around him, desperately calling upon the nullifying magic inside of me.

At first, it was hard to reach. The angel's repression spell kept it bound up inside me. But it didn't work perfectly on the nullifying magic since nullifying magic, by its very nature, would break down magic that tried to touch it. I could feel the power as a faint spark inside my chest.

I called upon it, forcing it to grow inside myself. It was faint at first. I squeezed my eyes shut, trying to ignore the outside world as it whipped by me. I forced the nullifying magic to grow, then pushed it toward Declan.

I had no idea if my plan would work, but I gave it my all, trying to use my magic to nullify the spell that bound Declan's own magic. The spell that bound his wings. It could just as easily bind his own magic, but since we were screwed anyway, it was worth a try.

"It's working." His voice was low and rough, likely from the effort of trying to call upon his wings.

I could feel the effort. The strain.

My heart thumped in my chest, loud as a drum. Finally, Declan's wings burst free. They flared, huge and glorious, behind his back. I clung to him as we shot upward, no longer falling.

In control of our fate.

I laughed, nearly hysterical, as Declan began to fly us toward the ground.

"Holy fates, that was insane," I said between gasps.

"You saved us."

"*We* saved us. And Wally." For all I knew, the hellcat was still up there, knocking over statues with ferocious glee.

"We're right over Magic's Bend. Look down."

I did as he said, my jaw dropping at the sight of the city sprawled out below us. Dusk was falling, and the lights were starting to come to life, making Magic's Bend look like a blanket of stars butting up against the sea.

Declan's strong arms tightened around me, and I looked up at him.

Holy fates, he was handsome.

And he'd risked so much for me.

"You knew they would catch us, didn't you?" I asked.

"I had a feeling. No one has ever successfully broken into—and gotten out of—the Heavenly Archives alive."

"Why didn't you tell me?"

"Would it have mattered? You'll die if we don't find this bastard and get the cure."

"Yeah, but you wouldn't."

He shrugged. "I wasn't worried about that."

Emotion made it feel like my heart had expanded in my chest, a sensation that was both lovely and extremely uncomfortable.

I was really starting to feel something for Declan, and damn, it was weird.

Feelings sucked.

I tried to ignore them as we landed on the roof of his building. When my legs finally hit solid ground, a low laugh of relief escaped me. I stumbled away from Declan, grateful to no longer be in the clouds.

"Let's get off this roof," he said.

"Best idea I've heard all day."

He led us toward the door, and I felt even better as I entered the stairwell and descended to his apartment. It would be a long time before I liked bridges again. Probably forever.

We stumbled into his apartment, both of us on shaky legs.

"Can I get you a drink?" he asked.

"Definitely. Something strong." I followed him to the kitchen, where he poured us each a glass of whiskey with no ice.

I wasn't a huge whiskey fan, but I slugged it back with gusto. It burned my throat as it went back, but it was so worth it.

I sighed and leaned against the counter. "I'm not normally into drinking my feelings, but I needed that."

"Me too." He looked out the window. "The sky is usually my favorite place to be. But that? That would give anyone anxiety."

I nodded. "Couldn't agree more."

He reached into his pocket and pulled out the paper that he'd torn from the book. I approached and leaned over his arm, stealing a peek at the smudged ink.

"I still can't make anything out." I frowned, squinting.

"Beyond the damage, I think it's in another language. So that's two things against us."

"You got anything in that uber high-tech room of yours that can help us?"

"I do, in fact."

I smiled. "Perfect. Let's go check it out."

His stomach grumbled, and the noise made me realize that I was also famished.

"How do you feel about cold pizza?" he asked. "I can get something fancier if you want, but that's what I have on hand."

"I feel *extremely* good about it. Under normal circumstances. Right now? It sounds like heaven."

He winced.

I frowned. "Yeah, bad choice of words." Heaven hadn't treated us so well.

Declan grabbed a box of pizza from the fridge, along with two refillable glass bottles of water.

I eyed them. "Into the environment, are you?"

He nodded. "When you can fly above the ocean, you're able to see all the plastic floating in it. Changed the way I think about things."

That made sense. And I admired it. I'd never been great about that kind of thing myself, but he made me want to try harder.

And I would. As soon as I cured myself and Mari of this damn curse. Even now, it was burning through my veins. I tried to shove the thought aside and followed him to the room in the back.

Right before I entered, my comms charm came to life.

"Aeri?" Mari's voice carried through static.

"Mari! How are you?"

"Weakening, but still going. We think we're onto something."

"What did you find?"

"A clue about—"

Static cut her off, and I tapped the charm. "Mari? Are you there? Mari?"

No sound. Crap.

Declan, who stood in the doorway, turned back to me.

I shrugged. "She thinks she's onto something, but she's somewhere with magical interference. My comms charm keeps cutting out."

"She's doing all right? With the curse?"

"Weakening, but all right." Just like I was. The curse dragged at me, fire burning in my veins. I ignored it and followed Declan into the control room.

The computer monitors and magical devices all blinked and flashed with different colors. Declan set the pizza and water on the table, and I grabbed a slice and bit into a cold pepperoni and mushroom. The water was icy and refreshing, and the combo helped settle some of the nerves that were still going wild inside me.

Declan polished off a slice of pizza in record time as he approached a fancy gizmo on the left wall. Vials of colorful potions were positioned around a platform in the middle. Glass tubes extended from the potions toward the center of the platform, joining in the middle and pointing downward toward the center. Tiny candles sat beneath the potions, their wicks blackened and burned.

"What does this do?" I asked, keenly interested in the potions.

"If it works as I intend, it will help us recreate what was written on this paper. It can turn back time for an object."

"Wow." My eyes widened as I inspected the vials of potion. "These can do that?"

"When used together, yes. It's the smoke that does it."

I looked at him with newfound appreciation. I knew he was a genius, but it was dawning on me how *much* of a genius. The way he experimented with this stuff was similar to the way Mari and I experimented with our blood sorcery potions.

I liked having that in common. We could learn a lot from each other.

Declan laid the paper on the platform between the potions, then drew a lighter from his pocket and lit each of the candles. They burned with an extra hot blue flame, causing the potions in the vials to boil and steam. The steam filled the glass tubes, then filtered toward the middle of the platform, where they formed a fog over the top of the paper.

I held my breath as I watched.

Slowly, the fog dissipated enough that I could see the paper. The black ink that obscured the writing faded, and golden writing began to form, scrolling and ornate. The writing was now legible, but like Declan had said, the language made it impossible to read.

He raised a cell phone and snapped a picture "The spell won't last long. Maybe a few more seconds. Once that mist totally disappears, the paper will revert to normal."

The words had barely left his mouth before the scrolled writing began to disappear. The smudges on the paper were all that remained.

"It shows an image of what it looked like in the past, then?" I asked.

"Exactly. It doesn't turn back time so much as reveal what once was."

"Cool."

Declan raised his phone and peered at the image. "Let's put this into Google."

I smiled. A little regular technology to go with all the fancy magical stuff. I liked the mix.

We each grabbed a second slice of pizza as we sat down in front of a computer. It took a few searches before we got lucky.

"Jackpot," Declan said. "It's a version of Old French—I thought it looked vaguely familiar—that says that we need to go to the SuperLouvre, in Paris. There will be a painting called The Fall there."

"The SuperLouvre?"

"A magical version of the human museum."

I leaned back in my chair. We had a location. Another piece of the puzzle.

Thank fates.

Relief flowed through me, followed quickly by a searing pain and weakness.

I sagged in my chair, curling over on myself.

Oh fates.

The curse.

It was like adrenaline had kept me going, and now that it was fading, the curse could roar to the forefront.

"Aeri." Declan turned to me, concern on his face. "Are you all right?"

"Fine." My voice was a croak.

"You're not. Is it the curse?"

I nodded. Every inch of me felt like it was on fire. Like I was being burned from the inside out. It had hurt before, but oh fates, this was awful.

"What can I do?" He sounded frantic.

I knew I wasn't supposed to take much of the potion that held off the effects, but I couldn't even move. The curse was so strong that it was incapacitating me.

"Potion. Right front pocket." The words took all my effort.

Declan went immediately for the pocket on my pants, but it was hard for him to access with the way I was curled over on myself. Finally, he pulled the potion free and uncorked it.

With his help, I drank half of it, then turned my head away. Too much of that stuff could kill me as surely as the curse itself.

Slowly, the agony began to fade.

I began to uncurl from my rolled-up position. Every muscle felt weak.

"Can I pick you up?" Declan asked.

"Why?"

"To help you lie down."

Okay, that actually sounded delightful. "Yes."

Carefully, he picked me up, treating me as if I were made of crystal. Just touching him made me feel better, and with every second that passed, my strength returned.

He carried me to a bedroom and laid me on the bed. By the time I hit the mattress, I was feeling almost normal. It was an illusion, of course. The curse still roared through me, but the potion had repressed it.

For now.

Fates, I hoped Mari was okay.

Declan stood over me in the bed, looking worried and extremely uncomfortable.

"What's wrong?" I asked. "You look...not so good."

He scrubbed a hand over his face. "I don't like feeling like there's no way to help, I guess."

My brows rose.

"Don't look so surprised," he said. "I've made it clear how I feel about you. Of course I want to help."

I shifted in the bed, then patted the spot next to me. "You can sit with me. That would help."

Immediately, he did as I asked, sitting next to me on the bed. I shifted farther left so I wouldn't be touching him. I didn't want the nullification magic making him ill.

He moved until his shoulder pressed against mine. Heat roared through me at even that small touch.

For fate's sake, it was just shoulder to shoulder.

That was nothing.

At least, it *should* have been nothing.

It was definitely not nothing.

My whole system went haywire when I touched him. The chemistry that was so strong between us roared to life, nullifying magic be damned. I could feel every inch of him. And from the way his muscles tightened, he could feel me.

I looked at him. "It doesn't bother you to touch me? You don't feel ill?"

Despite the fact that his face was slightly pale, there was heat in his yes. "Not enough to stop me from wanting to touch you. So no, it doesn't bother me."

"Really?"

"Want me to prove it?"

My mind raced. My heart thundered. Then, unable to help myself, I shrugged. "Yeah, prove it."

He pulled me toward him, his mouth swooping down on mine. I gasped, my hands going immediately to his shoulders. His lips moved expertly, driving all rational thought from my head.

His hands swept down my sides, his big palms leaving a wake of fire in their path. His mouth moved from my lips to the side of my neck, lighting up my nerve endings as he trailed kisses to my shoulder. He reached the crook of my neck and bit down, just hard enough to make sensation flash all the way through my body.

I pressed myself closer to him, feeling every inch of his hardness. A low moan tore from my throat, and I moved, letting instinct take over. Declan groaned, a harsh sound that lit me up from the inside.

When his hands ran down to my ass, I became an inferno. There was nothing to me but heat and desire. I tore his shirt off, running my palms over the hardness of his muscles. Visions raced through my head—images of us, doing everything two people could do in a bed.

And I wanted to.

Oh, how I wanted to.

What if this curse killed me and I never got the chance?

The thought ignited a fire of urgency beneath me. No way I was going to die without getting to sleep with Declan.

I tore my mouth from his and yanked my shirt over my head. My bra went next, and the desire in Declan's eyes made me shiver.

I reached for his belt, pulling the leather free of the loops. The snaps were even quicker, and Declan groaned.

"We're doing this?" he asked.

"Oh, we're doing this."

Declan grinned, a sexy smile that made the fire inside me burn ever brighter. We collided in an explosion, desire driving me wild.

An hour later, I lay with my head on his shoulder, exhausted.

"Wow." I blinked into the darkness of the room.

"I second that." His voice was rough.

"That was amazing." *The things he could do with his mouth.*

"I second that as well."

I leaned up to look at him. Though it was mostly dark in the room, I could still make out the paleness of his features.

Something withered inside me, and I pulled back, lying on the pillows so I didn't touch him.

As much as he wanted me and was determined to ignore the effects of my nullifying magic, he couldn't. It would always make him feel like shit.

"We can't do this again," I said.

"Sure we can."

"It makes you feel like crap."

He shrugged.

"I know you're willing to try to live with it," I said. "But I'm not."

"So don't."

"What do you mean?"

"I'd never ask you to give up magic that could save your life. That *has* saved your life. But you could learn to control it. To repress it when you don't need it."

I frowned at him. "That's not how a nullifier's magic works."

"You're right. But you're not a full nullifier. You just have a little bit of the power."

He had a point. If I'd possessed a full nullifier's power—for example, if I'd stolen it, which I wasn't even capable of—then it would repress all my other magic. It would make me feel like a walking corpse.

But it didn't, because I'd created only a small bit of it when I'd needed it.

"Do you really think it's possible?" I asked.

"I think it's worth trying."

Uncertainty filled me. As if he could sense it, Declan turned to look at me.

"I'm not sure," I said.

"Are you using it as an excuse to avoid this?" He gestured between us.

"I haven't avoided anything. I'm naked, after all."

"I mean the emotions, and I think you know it."

I scowled at him. Damn him, I hated that he was so insight-ful. Yeah, maybe I was avoiding getting close. I'd never truly, deeply trusted anyone except Mari. At best, I *mostly* trusted my friends the FireSouls. Logically, I knew I could trust them one hundred percent. But deep in my heart, I was still a weirdo about things like this. Mari and I had been betrayed by too many people we cared about to easily start trusting again.

If I pursued things with Declan, I'd definitely be opening myself up to hurt I didn't want to feel.

"Let me think about it," I said.

He frowned at me, but settled back on the pillows.

Smart guy. There was no point poking me when I was feeling like this, and I appreciated that he recognized that.

As I settled down next to him to go to sleep, I couldn't help but wonder where this would go. If I lived, could I handle it?

A terrified part of me said maybe not.

9

A SHRIEK TORE ME FROM SLEEP.

I sat bolt upright, panting. It took my panicking mind a few seconds to process where the noise was coming from.

"Aeri!" Mari's voice whispered out of the comms charm around my neck.

I slapped my hand to it. *That was* where the shriek had come from.

"What's wrong?" Ice chilled my skin.

"Abducted." There was static, something I'd never heard before on our comms charm. "Fallen angel." Dead silence now.

Fallen angel.

The word made fear sear through my veins, hot and fierce and driving away the ice of dread.

"Mari! Mari!" I hissed the words. "Are you okay? Where are you?"

"With Del." Static. "There's water nearby. I hear it."

Nothing. Silence.

"Mari!" I wanted to scream her name, but knew I couldn't. If she was hiding the existence of the comms charm—which she would do, since she was smart—I didn't want my shrieking voice to reveal its existence.

Silence.

There was nothing but dreaded, terrifying silence.

I turned to Declan, who sat up in bed beside me.

Terror made my insides feel hollow.

This couldn't be happening.

He reached for my hand and squeezed. "We'll find her."

"How?" The agonized words tore from my throat. "We have almost no info."

Before he could speak, I pulled my hand from his and tumbled from the bed. I didn't know where we'd start. But I had to do *something.*

"She was taken by Acius. We already have a clue to help track him. Once we find him, we'll find her."

I clung to his words like a lifeline. He was right. I knew he was.

I drew in a steadying breath.

This was the worst thing in the world—losing Mari.

I haven't lost her yet.

But it was my greatest fear come true. If I let it, the terror would dissolve me.

"Okay, we need to get started." I began tugging on my pants. "Shit."

"What?"

"I need to call the FireSouls." I scrambled for my pants and pulled the cell phone out of my pocket. They didn't have comms charms that connected to mine, though they did wear their own to talk to each other.

A wordless prayer raced through my mind as the phone rang. The FireSouls could find pretty much anything.

Maybe they could find Del and Mari.

Finally, Nix picked up. "Aerdeca?"

The panic in her voice told me that she already knew.

"Can you find them?" I asked immediately.

"No." Frustration echoed in her voice. "They're hidden by some kind of charm, I think."

I explained what we knew about Acius, and how he was the one responsible.

"So they're concealed by whatever charm hides him." Nix cursed.

"We've got a clue and we're tracking him."

"Good. We're going to keep hunting for Del. We'll check Grimrealm first. If we spread out and happen to get close enough to him, our power might be strong enough to break through the protection charm."

Fates, I prayed they could manage it. Their powers were stronger when they were closer to what they sought, and it wasn't unreasonable to think that Mari and Del might be in Grimrealm. That place was huge, but any direction was better than none, and we needed to spread out our forces.

"Good luck," Nix said.

"You too." I felt more connected to her than I ever had. As if the very thin wall of ice that I'd put up between us was melting.

She hung up before I could say anything, and I wasn't sure what I would have said anyway.

I hung up and looked at the time. Nearly midnight. We hadn't gotten a lot of sleep, but I was feeling well enough to get going. Not that it mattered. I could have felt like death warmed over and I'd be getting the hell on with the hunt.

I yanked the rest of my clothes on, then sat to put on my boots.

Declan yanked a shirt over his head. "Ready?"

I stood. "Yeah, let's get out of here. Should be about dawn in Paris. Hopefully it's not light yet."

"I've got a transport charm." He walked to the side table and picked up the small charm.

"You keep one on your bedside table?"

"Great for making an escape in a pinch."

I liked how he thought. It was dire, but it was smart. "Good. I have another so we can get out of there when it's all over."

"I'd bet good money we can't transport directly out of the museum."

I nodded. He had a point. If I owned a museum, I'd definitely enchant it so thieves couldn't easily sneak out with the goods.

Declan gestured to me. "Come on. Let's go."

I joined him near the bed.

He threw the transport charm to the ground. A cloud of gray, sparkling smoke burst upward. I gripped his hand, and we stepped inside. The ether sucked me in and tossed me through space, making my head spin.

When it spat us out in Paris, I nearly stumbled in the narrow alley. The night was still mostly dark, but the faintest bit of light was creeping over the horizon. Dawn would come soon.

"Good choice," I said as I inspected the narrow, brick-walled alley. No one had seen us arrive.

"We should be close to the museum." Declan went left, and I followed, arriving on a two-lane street that was nearly devoid of cars at this hour. Ornate street lamps shed a watery glow on the historic facades of the buildings.

I'd only ever been to the supernatural district of Paris once. It was in an older part of town, with beautiful buildings that just screamed *Fantasy Paris Vacay.*

There was a seedy underbelly, like in all magical neighborhoods, but on the surface it was lovely. Supernaturals liked to visit Paris just as much as humans, but we tended to stay in our own neighborhood. Hotels, cafes, and bars lined the street, most of them quiet. The smell of coffee and fresh French bread made my mouth water.

As if a bored god had heard my stomach grumble, fate blessed me.

A man walked down the street carrying a basket of French bread. The long loaves were wrapped in brown paper and smelled like actual heaven.

He neared us, and Declan spoke. "*Combien coûte une baguette, s'il vous plaît?*"

"*Deux euro.*"

Declan dug into his pocket and handed over a five-dollar bill. "*Gardez la monniae.*"

I looked at Declan curiously.

"Keep the change." He murmured the translation. "Since it's not exactly proper currency here."

The man looked at it, considering, then nodded and handed over the long loaf of bread. He sauntered away whistling, then turned into a coffee shop, no doubt making a delivery for the morning.

Declan tore the bread in half and handed me a long piece.

"You're a hero."

"It'd be better with butter and coffee, but this will have to do."

I bit into the bread, tearing off a piece. I covered my mouth as I asked, "Which way?"

My usual manners went totally to the wayside when presented with fresh bread and a growling stomach. The curse seemed to make me hungrier. Not to mention, we didn't have a lot of time.

Declan pointed down the street, towards a series of tall, ornately decorated stone buildings. We ate as we walked, moving at a swift clip. The sky was turning a dusky gray with dawn, and I wanted to get into the museum before the sun was up.

I ate quickly, polishing off the bread as we approached the front of the museum. It had once been an old Gothic church, complete with flying buttresses, gargoyles, and glittering glass windows. I searched the facade, looking for a weak point, but even from where we stood, I could feel the strong protection charm.

"I think we should go in from the top," Declan said.

"Fly?" I wasn't sure how I felt about that at this time of day, in the middle of a city that was waking up.

He frowned. "No. Too light. We'll draw too much attention." He pointed toward a narrow alley that separated the museum from the bank next to it. "We can climb up the wall in there. No one should see us."

I approached the alley to scope it out.

The space was narrow and dark. There were windows on the church side—it was far older than the bank, and I imagined this side had once had a view of the city. When the bank had gone up, they hadn't bothered putting in windows. There was only a few feet between it and the church, so there was nothing to see.

"Too narrow to fly," Declan said. "But the building is ornate enough that we can climb."

He was right. All of the decorative windowsills and carvings gave ideal handholds for scaling the wall. This would be *much* better than scaling the buildings in the Heavenly Archives.

I brushed off my hands and tilted my head back, searching for my route. "Top floor?"

He nodded. "Should be fewer protections up there."

"Race you to it." Normally, I'd find that to be quite fun. But even as the words left my lips, they felt hollow.

Mari.

Nothing was fun when Mari was at risk.

So I started climbing, hand over hand as fast as I could go. As we moved higher up, the building got smaller. A patio gave way to a dome, and I continued to climb, passing stone statues and gargoyles.

I was nearly to the top when magic flared to life. It pricked sharply against my skin, the only warning before the gargoyle next to me came to life and lunged. The stone monster was fast, and his big hand had slammed onto my back before I could even process what was going on.

"Trespasser," he growled.

I craned my neck to look back at him, catching sight of a mean stone face and a heavy brow. Horns the size of my forearm protruded from his head.

Shit.

My heart thundered, and sweat formed on my brow.

His big hand pushed harder against my back, threatening to crush my ribs against the stone wall. To my far right, I could see Declan making his way to me as fast as he could. He might trigger a gargoyle, too, and then we were both screwed.

An ache pounded in my chest as the gargoyle pressed harder.

I pushed backward, using my strength to try to gain a bit of breathing room. But the damned gargoyle was even stronger than me. Despite the pressure, my heart beat frantically.

There was no way that strength would save me.

I drew in a breath—not a deep one, since the gargoyle had just decreased the capacity of my lungs by about half—and called upon my magic. The new nullifying power was coming in horrifyingly handy, and if it saved me here, there was no way I could ever justify getting rid of it.

If that were even possible.

I let the power fill me, pushing it out and into the gargoyle. It was a spell that had brought him to life—something that I'd triggered when I'd gotten near him.

I just had to nullify that spell.

I used the crushing pain to fuel my magic, feeding it into the gargoyle.

Come on. Come on.

I felt it when the magic finally worked.

The gargoyle stilled, turning back to stone. And trapping me against the wall.

Shit.

I hadn't thought of that.

I was still trapped. He was no longer crushing me into the wall, but I was good and stuck.

"Hang on." Declan's low voice came from my right. "I'll break his arm off."

"No! He's historic."

"He's crushing you."

"Well, that too. But there's got to be a better way than breaking him." My mind raced, finally lighting on an idea. "Okay, here's what we'll do. I'm going to retract my nullifying magic."

"Control it, you mean?"

I knew what he was saying. He wanted me to practice repressing the magic so I could learn to do it all the time. So we could be together without him being sick. He knew I wouldn't stay with him as long as I made him ill.

"Whatever," I said. Now wasn't the time to discuss it. "Once I've retracted it and he comes back to life, he'll be pliable. Yank his hand off me, and I'll freeze him again. Then we can slip away."

"Fine. Good plan."

I drew in a fraction of a breath, then called on my nullifying magic, trying to suck it back into my body. It wasn't the same as fully repressing it, but it was sort of similar.

It took a moment, and a bit of effort, but finally I could feel the magic flowing back into me like a mist. I gathered in up inside me, envisioning it as a ball that I shoved down deep.

The gargoyle growled, the first sign of life, and the pressure on my chest disappeared as Declan yanked the gargoyle's arm back. Quickly, I reached back with my free hand and touched the gargoyle's stomach so I could feed the nullifying magic back into him.

From the corner of my eye, I could see Declan struggling with the gargoyle. His face was red and his brow creased. I was damned strong myself—supernaturally so—and I hadn't stood a chance against the gargoyle. Declan and the beast were both so strong that it was insane.

I sucked in a breath and fed my magic into the gargoyle, trying to force him to absorb the nullifying magic that would turn him to stone. I felt it flowing through him, until finally, he froze.

Declan dropped his hands, panting. "That was close."

I didn't remove my hand. As soon as I stopped feeding the magic into him, my hold on him would cease. He could very well come back to life.

I looked at Declan. "Why don't you go scout out an entry? Once you find one, I'll get away from this guy as fast as I can. Hopefully the nullification will hold for long enough that I can get away from the trigger."

I figured there had to be a radius of space around the gargoyle that would trigger him to come alive. If I could move fast enough, I could hopefully avoid it and him.

Declan gave me a look that made it really clear he wasn't fond of my plan. I knew him well enough by now to say that leaving me to get smashed again was low on his list of faves.

"You know it's the only way."

His scowl deepened, somehow making him more handsome —which annoyed me—but he nodded and began to climb. I kept my hand pressed to the gargoyle's chest and my magic flowing as I watched Declan.

We were at a flat section of wall where there were several windows. One of them had to let us in. I could feel protective magic grow as he checked each one, until finally, he managed to open one. His muscles strained as he pushed against the protective magic that kept the window closed. If he weren't so freaking strong, we wouldn't have a chance.

Finally, it opened. He looked down at me and nodded.

I gave the gargoyle one last look—and a final blast of nullification magic—and climbed up the wall as fast as I could. I was probably about seven feet away from the gargoyle when I heard his growl.

Shit!

My magic had faded.

I scrambled faster, glancing back to see the gargoyle lunge upward for me, one big arm outstretched. Next to me, Wally appeared, sitting on top of a windowsill. He leaned over and blasted a fiery red blaze at the gargoyle.

I didn't waste my chance. As Wally barbecued the stone monster, I climbed as fast as I could, trying to get far enough away that I would no longer trigger the spell that brought the stone beast to life.

"You're good." Declan's soft voice came from above.

I looked up. I was almost to him, thank fates.

A quick glance below showed that the gargoyle had frozen once again, this time in the reaching position he'd been in when he'd tried to grab me a second time. His stone form was blackened from Wally's fire, but otherwise he was unharmed.

Wally looked up at me from the windowsill, his fiery red eyes glued to me. *You're welcome. I take payment in the form of heated cat beds.*

"Fair enough." I nodded at him. "Soon as I get Mari back, I'll hop online and order the finest."

Online? Wally's whiskers twitched. *You can't get the fires of hell online.*

"You want a cat bed that's heated with the fires of hell? Electricity isn't good enough for you?"

He gave me a disparaging look and didn't bother responding.

"You're right, pal. What was I thinking? Crazy of me."

He nodded, then disappeared.

"I don't know what he was saying to you," Declan said. "But I think you should listen. That cat is useful."

"He wants some hellfire for his bed."

Declan frowned. "That's a tall order."

"No kidding." I peered into the window, spotting an administrative office that was stuffed full of books and binders. A computer sat on the desk, nearly buried beneath an avalanche of loose paper.

The window was only open about eighteen inches—probably because the spell made it weigh about five hundred pounds. I tested it, trying to lift it a bit more, and it didn't budge an inch.

Declan shimmied through and landed gracefully on the floor. I followed, my approach silent, and crouched behind the desk. My eye caught on a pamphlet lying beneath the chair. Colorful blocks indicated that it was a map of the museum. I snagged it and opened it.

French.

My French was terrible.

Declan leaned over my shoulder to inspect the pamphlet, then pointed at a small blue block in the corner on the lower level. "There. It says that it's the angelic collection."

"It's four floors down, on the main floor." I perked my ears, listening for any noise. "There must be a skeleton crew of guards here, since the museum won't open for hours yet."

"Probably more magical security, as well."

I rose to my feet, silent and slow. He was right. There was no telling what would fill this museum. We'd need to be careful.

Together, we exited into the main hall. It was a narrow, unadorned space. The walls were simply painted, and it was impossible to tell how this space had been used before the church had been converted into a museum with administrative offices.

Fortunately, this floor was totally empty, as was the staff stairwell that we found about ten yards down the hall. We moved silently toward the ground floor, exiting out into an alcove that held the bathrooms. I could feel magic prickle on the air—definitely protection charms—but I couldn't identify them.

I debated using my suit for invisibility, but decided against it. Too dangerous if Declan couldn't see me, and I could always flip the hood up quickly if necessary.

We'd reached the entry to the main hall—a soaring space with a multi-tone marble floor—when a voice rang out. "*Attention, aux intrus!*"

10

———————

"*Attention, aux intrus!*"

I spun around, spotting a security guard standing behind me. He was tall and broad-shouldered, his hands sparking with flame.

Not your ordinary museum security guard. But then, this was no ordinary museum.

The guard hurled a fireball at me, and I dived left, hitting the ground hard and sliding on the marble.

The damned fireball zoomed around and freaking *followed* me.

It plowed toward me. At the last second, I rolled left. The fire plowed into the ground next to me, grazing my thigh.

Heat and pain flared.

Shit.

I called on my shield from the ether. Declan already had his out. He charged the guard. The tall mage threw another blast of fire at Declan. The fireball was the size of a dinner plate. When it slammed into Declan's shield, his approach slowed.

Crap, this guard was strong.

I surged to my feet and charged, following behind Declan.

The guard threw two more fireballs at us. I raised my shield just in time, and flame crashed into it, making my arms shake and nearly sending me backward.

I sprinted forward. Declan was in the lead, and he didn't stop running. He picked up the pace and smashed his shield into the mage, who went flying backward.

I sprinted up beside them, just in time to see Declan grab the mage and put him in a sleeper hold. The man slumped to the left, unconscious.

Panting, I crouched down. "Nice work."

"Didn't want to kill him. Guy is just doing his job."

"Trying to kill us."

"Which is part of his job."

"Fair enough." I grabbed the cuffs that were pinned to the guard's belt. "Aren't these handy?"

Declan gathered the man's wrists, and I snapped the cuffs on. Then I undid his tie and gagged him.

"I've got him." Declan stood and hoisted the mage over his shoulder. The guy had to weigh at least two hundred pounds, but Declan picked him up like he was a feather and carried him to a small closet. He stashed him inside.

I stood and turned to inspect the foyer, my muscles tensed and ready to fight. Had another guard heard? Would there be more coming?

But this place was *huge*.

Depending on how many guards there were, they could be off in wings where they didn't even hear the shout of "*Attention, aux intrus!*" After a few seconds, when no one else showed up, I figured the coast was clear.

Quietly, I approached the entrance to the main hall.

All of the exhibits led off this massive, three-story open space, but there was no way we'd be able to just waltz through.

That was too easy.

I didn't trust easy.

I crouched low and inspected the walls, eying the wooden trim near the floor. It was ornately carved, so much so that it was almost impossible to see the imperfections. But I spotted them and grinned. Tiny holes were drilled every twelve inches, and a few of them glowed with a bright red light.

"See?" I pointed. "Lasers."

"Like in human museums."

I frowned. "I bet they really burn you though. A simple alarm system, sure. But supernaturals would go the extra mile."

I looked up, searching for more laser holes positioned higher in the room. "Can you see any above floor level?"

Declan searched the area for a while, then finally shook his head. "If there are any, I can't see them."

I looked at him. "That closet you stashed the guard in. Was it a cleaning closet?"

"Yeah."

"Hang on." I ran back to it.

The guard was still unconscious when I opened the door, but I found my target. A bottle of blue window cleaner. I snagged it, then returned to Declan.

He eyed it. "Smart thinking."

I grinned, then turned to the huge room. First, I sprayed the cleaner at the floor. It hissed when it hit the lasers, and they sparked red, fine little lines that were now visible in the mist.

"Test complete." I raised the bottle and sprayed upward.

Nothing hissed.

I sprayed slightly to the left, then the right. Then even higher.

Finally, there was a faint hiss and one single laser line appeared, about six feet over our heads. I looked at Declan. "Can you fly in that space?"

He frowned, considering, then nodded. "As long as there aren't many more laser lines, we should be okay."

"Can I hitch a ride?" I raised the bottle. "I'll spray."

"Anytime." He held out his arms, and I climbed into them, clinging close.

His wings flared behind his back, and a tiny little thrill raced through me. I looked up at him, catching sight of the paleness of his face.

Damn it.

My nullification magic.

I gripped the spray bottle tight and tried to ignore the distress that filled me. I hated that I made him feel that way. Even worse, he was determined to silently ignore it, which was all noble and lovely.

How was a woman supposed to resist that?

No woman could be expected to.

Slowly, I drew in a breath and tried to call upon my nullification magic. But instead of sending it outward to use it, I called it inward. I tried to shove it down deep to a place in my soul where it couldn't leak out and hurt Declan.

He stiffened slightly, then looked at me. "Are you doing that?"

"Doing what?" For whatever reason, I didn't want to admit it.

"You're repressing your magic."

"Don't know what you're talking about."

"I can feel it."

I shrugged. "Still don't know."

"Thanks," he said.

My shoulders relaxed, just slightly. It was one thing for me to try to make this step toward *more*. It was another thing to discuss it out loud—while breaking into a museum, for fate's sake, as if this was the place I wanted to explore my deepest feelings and personal growth.

I appreciated that he recognized that. I wasn't even fully committed to trying this with him. But there was no harm in at least trying to repress the nullification magic. It wasn't impossible like I'd thought, so it was worth exploring.

"Well, get going," I said, eyeing him.

He nodded, then took off into the air, slowly and delicately. I could feel the strain it took to fly at a specific height, but Declan managed it.

I leaned outward and sprayed the cleaner, trying to get it to travel as far as possible so we could see if lasers were in our path. Occasionally, the fine mist would hiss and crackle, and Declan would deviate.

My muscles tensed with every new laser I found, until I felt like I was wound so tight I would snap. At one point, we reached a sticky situation where a laser burned the edge of Declan's wing.

He winced and clutched me tighter.

"You okay?"

"Couldn't be better." The strain in his voice made me frown.

I sprayed and sprayed, feeling like the lamest part of this team with my window cleaner.

By the time we reached the other side, I was desperate to be on solid ground. Declan hovered in the air, and I sprayed the floor, finding it clear. The baseboards here were simple—not ornately carved to hide the laser holes—so it'd be safe throughout the whole room, probably.

Declan set me down, and I stumbled away on shaking legs. "Thank fates that's over."

Declan nodded and walked toward the entrance that marked the angelic collection. I followed him, and we both stopped in the archway, inspecting the room beyond.

Massive paintings filled the space, some over ten feet high and twenty feet wide. They were all ornately done, with the kind of moody colors that always seemed to accompany angel artwork. Well, moody except for the golden sky, which was always heavy with clouds and bright with gold light streaming through.

Magic sparked around the entrance to the room, and I hesitated. "There's another protection charm here."

"I feel it." Declan raised a hand midair and hovered it at the threshold to the other room. He winced. "Burns." He retracted his hand and inspected it, then showed me. "Not red."

"Just pain, then. No damage." I sucked in a deep breath. "Better get it over with."

I stepped into the room—or tried to, at least. My foot stopped at the threshold.

"You have to push," Declan said.

"Ah, just like the wall in the alley that leads to Grimrealm. But with added pain." I tilted my head. "Someone should tell the Grimrealm folks that pain is a possibility. I'm sure they'd love to upgrade."

A smile quirked the corner of Declan's mouth. "I'll leave that up to you."

"Yeah, I'll get right on it. Never." No more time to waste. I braced myself, then threw myself against the invisible threshold.

The pain burst against my skin, a horrible burning sensation that nearly made me shriek. It felt a hell of a lot like the fire that blasted through my veins when the fire veins curse got bad. So now I got to enjoy burning up from without *and* within.

Wasn't I a lucky girl?

It was incredibly hard to break through, and I shoved with all my might. Declan's strong hands pressed against my back, and he pushed me through, giving me the extra bit of strength to tumble through and onto the floor.

The pain faded almost immediately.

I turned to see Declan plow through the force field and land in a pile next to me.

I rolled over to face him, still aching slightly. "Thanks for the shove."

He nodded, sitting up slowly. "Why didn't you use your nullifying magic?"

"Don't want to waste it. With the way the curse is weakening me, I don't want to use magic unless I have to." Also, I felt a bit bad not feeling the fire if Declan had to. Which was *dumb*.

Of course I didn't say that. What was I, crazy?

Declan stood and reached for my hand. I let him pull me to my feet, then turned and inspected the room.

The painting was obvious as soon as I laid eyes on it. It sat at one end of the long gallery, dominating a wall all by itself. At least twenty feet tall and ten feet wide, it was a monster piece of artwork.

I walked closer, my eyes devouring the painting. An angel fell from the sky, looking for all the world like Lucifer, though I knew it was our man, Acius.

"That's him," Declan said.

I stopped in front of the painting, inspecting it. The angel was falling toward a building that was built onto an island. It sat in the middle of a dark blue sea, the fortress on top looking like an impenetrable place. Though the building was made of pale, sun-bleached stone, it somehow managed to look miserable.

The angel's wings were burning as he fell, a look of agony on his face.

"This was his fall," Declan said.

"Yours wasn't like that, right?" It looked *awful*.

"No. Mine wasn't nearly as bad. Whatever he did, it was evil." He leaned closer to the painting, inspecting the fortress. "Where is that place?"

I drew my phone from my pocket and snapped a picture. "I

think it's where we need to go next. The angel is clearly headed there."

Declan frowned.

"*Attention, aux intrus!*"

Shit.

I spun around to see a security guard racing toward us

"*Arrêtez!*" the guard shouted. "*Plus de gardes sont en route!*"

"He said that more are coming," Declan translated.

Crap. We needed a way out. Were we even done here? We had to be. I was sure the building in the painting was the clue, and I had a picture of it.

Now we just had to avoid getting caught by these guards.

Frantic, I looked left and right. There was an exit to our left. We needed to find a window or a door to the exterior of the building so we could use our transport charm.

The guard charged us, raising a flaming hand. Honestly, it was stupid to use fire mages as guards around all this valuable artwork. For that reason, he was clearly hesitating. As long as we stood in front of this painting, he wouldn't want to hurl fire at us.

A noise from the left caught my attention, and I turned.

Too late.

A guard stood there, clearly having just thrown something. I caught sight of a ruby red potion bomb the second before it slammed into Declan.

He went down like a sack of bricks.

I drew a knife from the ether and hurled it at the guard, nailing him in the shoulder, right about the heart. He collapsed.

The other guard was nearing us. I had to take him out, but I wanted to check on Declan.

A half second later, Wally appeared. The little black shadow raced toward the approaching guard, a blast of red flame bursting from his mouth.

I dropped to my knees next to Declan and pressed my finger-tips to his throat. A pulse.

Relief swept through me.

As Wally chased the guard around the huge room, I surged upward and grabbed Declan's arm, then dragged him toward the exit. I passed the guard's bleeding body in the narrow archway without feeling an ounce of guilt. I didn't know what he'd hit Declan with, but it could be deadly.

Fair's fair.

I dragged Declan into a corridor. There was a stained glass window that probably led onto an alley. At least, that was my guess, given the minimal amount of light flowing through. Magic pulsed from it, a strong protective charm that would make the window difficult to break.

It hadn't met me yet.

I dropped Declan's arm and called my mace from the ether. I swung it fast, several times around to get good momentum, then slammed it through the glass. The colorful design shattered, and I ducked my head.

I could hear an enraged shriek from inside the gallery. Probably the guard.

And while I did feel a *little* guilty about damaging the build-ing, it was either that or death. I'd take property destruction any day.

As I'd suspected, there was an alley on the other side of the window. Thank fates we were on the ground floor. We were probably even on the same side of the building that we'd entered through.

I sucked in a deep breath and crouched, pulling Declan up into a fireman's carry. I grunted as his weight settled on my shoulders.

"Damn, you're dense," I muttered as I staggered through the broken glass window, careful to avoid the shards that stuck upright. Once in the alley, I gripped both of Declan's hands with one of my own, making sure to keep him on my back, then dug into my pocket with the other.

I withdrew the transport charm and slammed it onto the ground, imagining heading for Magic's Bend. The sparkling gray cloud burst up, and I stepped through, calling back to Wally as I left. "Thanks, pal! We're out of here!"

I heard a yowl, which I assumed to be a goodbye, since nothing could hurt Wally. The ether sucked me up and spit me out on the street in Darklane. On instinct, I'd gone straight to my house. It was still dark, and I dropped Declan onto a patch of grass, then knelt by his side and smacked his cheek lightly.

"Come on, wake up." Worry tugged at every ounce of me as I watched him. "Come on!"

He groaned and moved his head, his eyes slowly blinking open.

"You okay?"

He raised a weary hand and rubbed his face. "What happened?"

"Guard hit you with a sedative. At least, I think it was a sedative." I inspected him. He looked all right, at least. "Can you walk?"

"I can try." He staggered upright with my help. "Legs are wobbly, but fine."

"Good. Come on. We need to go check out that clue. I want to find out what that building in the painting is called."

He nodded and followed me up the stairs. "Thanks for getting me out of there."

"Anytime."

I disengaged the locks and security charms, then stepped into the foyer. "Let's eat while we do this."

My bright white kitchen welcomed us, and I went immediately to the bell that sat on the counter. I rang it twice to let the

Jade Lotus know we wanted food, then grabbed two cups of water and returned to the table where Declan had collapsed into a chair.

"That was some serious stuff," he said.

"If you're not feeling better after food, I'll get you a potion." From behind me, the bell rang. "Speaking of."

I turned to see the portal that sat right over the counter spit out two cartons of Chinese food. I grabbed them, along with some chopsticks, and brought them back to the table. I gave one to Declan, then dug into my own as I pulled up the photo on my phone.

"The image is pretty clear," I said. "I'm going to crop out the building and put it into Goggle reverse image search."

We ate as I worked, my stomach roiling with nerves. I was hungry—sort of—but more than that, I needed to keep my strength up if I wanted to save Mari. Even now, the fire in my veins was burning. This damned curse got worse with every hour, so how was Mari feeling?

Like shit, probably.

If she's still alive.

At the thought, my stomach lurched so hard that I nearly vomited. I sucked in a shaky breath and tried to banish the thought.

Don't go there.

I would get to her in time. I had to. I *had* to.

Finally, my phone pulled up a match. I looked at Declan, who already appeared improved. "Have you heard of the Chateau d'If? In France?"

He frowned, clearly searching his memory. "It's a prison, right?"

I nodded. "A very famous one. A very deadly one, full of the worst demons and mages in the world. Not that I can understand why they bother imprisoning them if they can just kill them."

He raised a brow.

"What? I'm a demon slayer. Slaying demons is what I do. It's in the job title."

"If a regular person kills them, they just get sent back to their underworld. They could escape again."

"Good point. I guess they don't have a slayer on staff." We were the only ones who could kill them for good, and I knew I wouldn't be volunteering for the job of executioner. It was one thing to hunt them myself when I knew exactly the evil deeds they'd committed.

Just waiting for demons to show up so I could lop their heads off didn't sound very appealing.

That was yet another good reason to hide what I was. No way I wanted to be shanghaied into a job at a prison, chopping off demon heads night and day.

"They could also be in holding in case they have skills or knowledge that is needed."

"Fine, fine. I see your point." I clicked through the link. "There's very little info on here. Most sources agree that it's a myth."

Declan shrugged. "Goggle is run by humans. It's a supernatural prison. We're lucky they know that much."

I nodded as I squinted at the two images on my little phone screen. The prison building was ancient. Eight hundred years old, at least. Maybe a thousand. I was no expert. But it looked like a castle sitting on top of a rock in the middle of the ocean.

"Supernatural Alcatraz," I said.

"And we're going to break in."

Somehow, this felt like a very bad idea.

But it was the *only* idea.

11

Declan and I didn't waste any time. We headed directly for my workshop, where I gathered up a bundle of potions. We'd need to be prepared.

First, I handed him an energy potion. We were running on too few hours of sleep. After we'd drunk them, I collected a variety of different potions that might come in handy when breaking into a prison.

I stashed them in a little bag, then stuck it in the ether.

Declan looked at me with wide eyes. "That's a useful spell. And rare."

I nodded. It cost a lot of money to stash something in the ether for later use. That was why it was primarily used for things like weapons, which you didn't use up. With something like potions that were used in one go, it was rarely considered worth it. I'd bought the enchanted bag last year, though, and it allowed me to store the potions for when I really, really needed them. Like all magic, the spell that enchanted it decayed with time— quite quickly, in this case—so I used it rarely.

"For this, it's worth it," I said. "Let me call Nix and Cass and update them on our progress, then we can go."

I made a quick phone call and found out they weren't much farther along. They'd ruled out several places in Grimrealm, but the whole place was a complicated labyrinth. It'd take them more time, and even then, there was no guarantee. They promised to come after us in twelve hours if we didn't get back in touch, though.

I hung up and looked at Declan. "Ready?"

"Let's do this."

We used a transport charm to get to the French fishing village that was supposed to be close to the prison island. When we arrived, the sun was nearing the horizon.

"Damn, we were in that museum for longer than I thought," I said.

Declan looked at the sky. "By the time we get a boat, it should be dark."

I inspected my surroundings. The little village crowded up against the dark blue sea, the white buildings ancient and charming. The scent of food wafted on the air from the seaside restaurants, and boats bobbed on the harbor.

"You'd have no idea there was a supernatural prison out there." I looked toward the sea, where the ruins on the island sat, buffeted by the waves. This town was a human town, and the ruins looked abandoned to the inhabitants. They'd probably been enchanted to repel people with the idea that they were unsafe. Any brave souls who dared approach were likely turned back by anxiety or something along those lines.

"There's a harbor that way," Declan said.

It would have been faster to fly to the island, but the humans definitely would have noticed.

We made our way across the town, sticking to the edge of the harbor. I passed by couples drinking wine at tiny tables and old women debating something over a pot of tea. Children played on a green square where a fountain burbled, and a cat rolled in the grass. It was all so lovely and normal.

"Freaking weird how Black Magic Alcatraz is spitting distance from this bucolic scene," I murmured.

Declan shook his head. "If those demons escaped..."

Just the idea was horrible. "Yeah, this prison is a terrible idea."

We reached the harbor as the sun dipped fully behind the horizon. The sky lit with a brilliant pink glow before descending into darkness. When the town lights began to sparkle on the waves, I looked at Declan. "It's as dark as it's going to get."

We found a little wooden boat tied at the end of the dock. There was a small chest sitting next to it on the little pier, and a name was inscribed on it.

"Piers Franz," I read. "He must own the boat."

I lifted up the lid of the box and found life jackets and other assorted boat paraphernalia.

Declan leaned over and dropped a few hundred dollars into the box. "Just in case we don't return it."

I smiled at him. "Good thinking."

Quickly, we climbed into the boat and untied it. Declan picked up the oars and began to row, and I scanned the shore, hoping that Piers or one of his friends weren't eating at a seaside restaurant. Last thing we needed was them witnessing our theft and setting up the alarm.

Fortunately, no one seemed to notice, and we were able to quickly row far from shore. Waves buffeted the little boat, crashing over the bow, but Declan kept us on a steady course. I eyed the looming structure as we approached. Part of it was a cliff that extended straight down into the sea, dropping a good thirty feet. The castle prison crouched on top. The other side of the island was a more gradual slope.

I searched for guards, but saw none who were watching the

sea. "I don't see anyone on guard."

"They're probably more concerned with those inside the prison than outside of it. I doubt they get many visitors."

"Good point." Who the hell would want to break *in* here?

Any person in their right mind would stay the hell away.

"Go to the left," I said, directing Declan to a good place to beach our little vessel. It was far enough from the main prison that hopefully no one was looking.

He rowed us right up to the rocky shore, and I leapt up and pulled the boat mostly out of the water. Declan climbed out and helped me haul the boat onto the shore and hide it behind some rocks.

"The whole place feels totally abandoned," I whispered.

"I doubt they leave the castle much. Wouldn't want to alert anyone to the fact that people live here."

"*Live* is a generous term."

A smile pulled up the corner of his mouth. I could barely see him in the faint moonlight.

"Come on." I turned and set off toward the castle.

We stuck close to the shore, reaching an area where the cliff rose high. There was a sturdy iron gate set into the base of the cliff, and an area to pull boats out of the water.

"This is our best bet," Declan murmured.

I nodded and pressed myself up against the cliff wall, then tiptoed toward the gate, making sure to stay out of view of anyone who could possibly be on the other side, looking out.

I got up close and listened intently. I could hear no one, so I peeked my head around and inspected the gate. It was massive, made of iron bars as thick as my arm. The whole thing was at least ten feet tall and eight feet wide. Within, a tunnel was faintly lit by old electric lights. Somehow the crappy flickering electricity illuminating the ancient cavern made the place even creepier.

I ducked back against the wall and looked at Declan, then whispered, "I think we—"

The sound of footsteps coming from within the tunnel made me shut my mouth.

It had to be a guard. He was leaving. Or looking for us, if he'd happened to hear or see us approach.

My mind raced. A plan formed.

I leaned close to Declan and pointed to a nearby bush, then quietly hissed, "Hide."

It was obvious from the look on his face that the idea was abhorrent, but I glared so hard that he listened. I waited until he headed toward the bushes and then flipped up my invisibility hood. Sure, my plan was dangerous. But at least I had one.

Declan darted behind the bush at the same time the guard opened the gate to peer out. I drew a dagger from the ether— one with a really heavy hilt—then slammed it into his skull.

He dropped like a rock, unconscious. Fortunately for us, his body propped the gate right open. Declan materialized at my side a moment later, silent as a cat.

Quickly, I tore a strip off the guard's shirt and bound his mouth. I searched his pockets for keys and took every one that I could find—four, total. Declan grabbed the iron cuffs at his wrists—iron, not steel, which I thought was a super old-school choice—and bound his wrists behind his back. Then he dragged him behind the bush while I held the gate open.

He returned and murmured, "That was efficient."

"Stick with me, pal." I slipped into the darkened tunnel.

Declan followed, quietly closing the gate behind us but not locking it.

Together, we made our way silently down the hall. The lights buzzed in my ear, giving this place a real torture-dungeon feel. We descended deeper underground as we traveled.

Finally, I began to hear voices. I slowed, listening carefully.

They sounded somewhat jovial.

"Not prisoners," I murmured.

We crept closer, peering out into a cavern that was carved into the earth. A pond in the middle rippled under the lights. It was a weird shape with little arms that flowed between the rock outcroppings in the space, and one part of it butted up against the rock wall. It even looked like the water might flow underneath.

On the far side, a table full of men sat and talked. Cards and food littered the table.

"Break time," Declan murmured.

Behind the men, there was a stairway leading up. Unfortunately, there were eight guards. Since they had been hired to contain the most dangerous demons and mages around, they had to be skilled.

"Too many to fight." If I had my choice, at least. "We'd lose our element of surprise."

"Maybe there's another way."

There were a number of natural rock outcroppings in the space, and we managed to creep behind some, working our way deeper into the cavern. It'd take time to search it all. Time that I wasn't sure I had.

Hey. You look sneaky.

I nearly jumped, then looked down at Wally. He'd appeared at my side, his smoky dark fur wafting up from him as his fiery eyes met mine. Next to him, a tiny black figure stood. He was also ephemeral, though he looked more like he was made of shadow than smoke.

I could feel the skepticism coming off the little figure, who couldn't be more than twelve inches tall. Some kind of sprite, I had to guess.

"Who's your friend?" I whispered, so low that Wally had to twitch his ears to hear.

Declan watched me.

Don't know his name. He's a shadow sprite. Lives here.

"Well, isn't that handy?"

The sprite glared at me. He didn't have facial features in the way I thought of them, but I could feel his annoyance.

"I don't think he likes me," I said.

Wally turned his head to look at the sprite, then looked back at me. *Nah, we're old friends. He likes you fine.*

"Old friends? How old?"

Ten minutes?

No point in arguing with Wally about the definition of old friendships. "Can he tell us another way to get up into the prison?"

Wally turned to the sprite. I couldn't hear him speak, but they did seem to be communicating. Finally, Wally turned back to me. *You can go up through the well.*

I grimaced. That sounded miserable.

"Saltwater well?" I pointed to the pond in the middle of the cave.

Wally turned back to the sprite to translate. A moment later, he looked at me. *Yes. That's the way.*

I sighed. Of course it was. At least there was an entrance to the water that was away from the guards. If we held our breath long enough and swam hard, we had a chance. But just to be sure, I asked how far the well entrance was.

Not far. Only a few meters. Just stay at the left edge where it is deep. There will be a dead-end, then you go up. It will be obvious.

Oh, that sounded like a load of crazy crap.

I translated for Declan.

"Sounds insane."

"But we don't have any other choice. Not unless we want to fight the guards and blow our cover."

"Agreed."

My heart thundered at the idea of swimming in that dark water, but I ignored it.

"You trust that little shadow sprite?" Declan asked.

"I trust Wally. And he'd probably eat the shadow sprite if he lied so..." I shrugged.

Declan sighed. "Good enough for me."

I patted his shoulder. "Excellent."

Since the little pond was a weird shape that stretched over this way, we were able to sneak into the water under the cover of one of the rock outcroppings. It was cold and horrible—not to mention dark.

Please don't let there be monsters.

It was deep like Wally had said it would be, and we were close to the edge where it disappeared under the vertical wall. The well should be in there, right behind the rock.

My heart roared in my ears, and I looked at Wally.

Wally met my gaze. *I trust the sprite.*

"You better." I gave him a wobbly smile, then sucked in a breath and ducked under the surface.

It was pitch black, so I kept my eyes closed. With one hand running along the rock wall to my left, I guided myself through the dark water. I estimated that I was at the part of the pool where I'd be exposed to the guards if I popped my head up.

I made sure not to kick too hard, just in case they looked over and spotted movement, and used my hand to drag myself along the rock wall. Prayers raced through my mind as I swam forward. I was swimming blind and I *hated* it.

This was not my idea of a good time in the water.

The scientific names of all the creepy things that could be in this water flashed in my mind.

Neoclinus blanchardi.

Idiacanthus atlanticus.

Gymnothorax javanicus.

I banished the thoughts of fishy fangs and fast swimmers.

Finally, the wall to my left hit a dead end.

Please work.

I kicked upward, my hand above my head to feel for the well entrance. Something brushed my legs, and bubbles escaped my mouth on a scream. I snapped my mouth shut.

Just Declan.

It was just Declan.

Not a monster.

My hand hit a solid surface above me. Frantic, I patted around, searching for the hole that would lead me up into the well. My lungs burned. I was running out of time.

Oh fates, this was bad.

Finally, I found the entrance. I shot upward, praying that really was a well and not a dead end.

Finally, my head broke through the surface and I gasped.

Stale air filled my lungs.

Best feeling ever.

The well stretched up high above me, showing a slice of the moon.

Declan surfaced next to me, gasping.

I whispered, "Well, that sucked."

He chuckled low in his throat. "Let's get the hell out of here."

I reached for the edge of a rough stone block that formed the edge of the well and began to climb. Hand over hand, I pulled myself out of the water until I could prop my feet on the wall. Then I shimmied up.

Declan followed, and we reached the top in record time. Mostly, I just wanted to get the hell away from that dark and murky water.

It'd give me nightmares, for sure. Hell, it had almost ruined swimming for me. When I reached the top, I carefully peeked the top half of my head out. Just enough to see.

We were in the middle of an ancient, open-air courtyard. It was basically a hole cut into the middle of the castle, surrounded on all sides by sturdy walls and a massive stone staircase that led upward to the second and third levels.

There wasn't a soul in sight, thank fates, and I seriously doubted these prisoners got yard time. This didn't strike me as a humane prison.

No, this courtyard was a relic of the past. The cells would be built into the walls of the building that surrounded it.

Quickly, I scrambled out and raced toward an alcove in the wall where I could hide. Declan followed, and we crouched in the shadows.

I leaned my shoulder against his.

"I'm not one for nightmares," he said, "but swimming blindly under a cliff would be good inspiration for some."

A smile cracked across my face as I studied the courtyard. We sat in silence for several minutes, waiting to see what kind of guard activity might happen. It was ancient and empty, though, with not a bit of movement to be seen.

Stone walls soared three stories tall on either side, with a few windows looking out onto the courtyard. Glass panes filled the windows instead of bars. Probably guards' rooms or offices.

"Ready to go exploring?" I asked. I had a feeling this whole place was an ancient maze. It'd take time to find what we were looking for. Especially since I didn't know exactly *what* we were looking for besides a clue as to Acius's whereabouts.

Declan nodded. "Stairs first?"

"That's what I was thinking." I raced out from behind the alcove and took the stairs two at a time, heading up to the second floor. The heavy wooden door at the top wasn't locked, and I slipped inside a dark, stone-walled hallway.

Declan was silent as he entered after me, and I pressed myself up against the wall as I moved toward the first door. I pressed an ear to it and heard nothing within, so I pushed at the ancient wood.

It creaked as it opened, revealing an office cluttered with papers. A coffee mug sat in the middle of the desk, and I looked over to peer in. An inch of cold coffee sat at the bottom.

"Admin office," I murmured.

Declan went to the ugly metal filing cabinets that lined the wall. "This place might be a supernatural prison, but they've still got admin. Maybe we can find prisoner records."

I nodded, liking how he was thinking. It was too dangerous to sneak around the prison without a goal in mind. Every second we walked the halls, we risked getting caught. Considering the fact that this place was meant to house the strongest and the worst, we'd have a hard time getting out if we were caught.

Instead of inspecting the contents of the filing cabinet, Declan went for the ancient-looking books piled on top.

"That painting made it look like he came here directly from headquarters, which was hundreds of years ago." He picked up one of the leather books and handed it to me, then took one for himself.

I leaned against the desk and began to rifle though, searching for the name Acius.

Though his name didn't appear immediately, others did.

Rictus the Devourer.

Cortas, Slayer of Men.

Diero the Putrid.

Vlad the Impaler.

I whistled low under my breath. "They've had quite the contingent of famous guests here."

"Including our guy." Declan held his open book out in front of him so I could look at the page.

I peered at the terrible, scratchy writing, my gaze finally landing on *Acius the Fallen, Cell Block Z.*

12

We'd found him.

Or at least, the place that he used to be.

I nodded and shut my book. "Good work."

We returned our leather-bound tomes to the top of the filing cabinet and made sure they looked just as they had when Declan had picked them up, then we slipped out into the corridor.

"Now we just need to find Cell Block Z," I murmured. We could have searched the office for a map, but nah. That was unlikely to exist for a prison as old as this one. And if you worked here, you knew where to go.

We crept through the halls, finally leaving the administrative section and reaching an area that was a lot less comfortable. Considering that the admin hall had consisted of barren floors, stone walls, and flickering electric lights, that wasn't saying much.

But this part...

It sucked.

The admin hall gave way to a small room that was clearly a

transitional room. It was barren and stone-walled, with a massive iron door on one side.

It reeked of misery and rage, most of which seemed to be coming from beneath the door.

The prisoners had to be on the other side.

I shared a look with Declan. "Remind me not to break any major laws, because I *don't* want to end up here."

He nodded, not mentioning that my very species—Dragon Blood—could lead me to a place like this if the government figured out what I was and thought I was misusing my gift to create too many dangerous powers.

That is, if they didn't want to use me for my power.

In the toss-up of being turned into a weapon and being thrown in a place like this, I guessed even this was the better option.

Man, my life is screwed up.

I approached the heavy door. "I wonder how many guards are on staff? We haven't seen a single one."

"Depends on how sturdy the cells are and if they ever let them out."

"My guess is very sturdy, and no, they never get out." I rested a hand against the iron door, feeling for any kind of protective charm.

Magic prickled my skin, feeling like tiny beestings. I yanked my hand away and debated. Declan was strong enough that he could probably break this door down, but I didn't want to alert anyone to our presence.

"I've got this." I reached into my pocket and pulled out the four keys I'd taken from the guard earlier.

The third one worked, and the lock snicked open. I pulled the door open a few inches and peered inside. A long, stone-walled hallway stretched out in front of me. It was mostly dark, lit only with flickering electric lights that buzzed in a way that would drive me mad after only thirty seconds. Cell doors lined the space, each about fifteen feet apart. Some were solid iron, others made of iron grate.

I shut the door and looked back at Declan. "Cells inside. I'm going to check it out while invisible. Can you wait here?"

He frowned. "I don't like it, but fine. Obviously."

I nodded and squeezed his shoulder, then flicked my hood up.

Invisible, I opened the door and slipped into the hallway.

Immediately, the cooped-up rage in the place hit me hard. My insides turned and my hair stood on end.

These folks are pissed.

The second feeling that hit me was one of helplessness. I blinked, taking a second to figure it out.

My magic was dampened. That was it.

Of course.

A prison for supernaturals would need some serious nullifying magic to keep them under control.

Silently, I crept down the hall. My heart thundered in my ears as I passed the first cells. Solid metal doors with one tiny window. I couldn't see in unless I got right up close to the glass. But they could look out.

I liked a good fight. I was damned skilled.

But I counted at least twenty cell doors. If they opened for any reason…

I couldn't hold my own against twenty of the world's most hardened criminal supernaturals. I'd be dead within a minute as they fought their way to escape.

I shivered and kept going, searching for any sign of which cell block this was. There were no markings on the doors—no numbers, letters, or names.

I passed the first cell that had metal bars instead of a solid door. A small demon lay asleep on a narrow bed. He looked harmless. Except for the purple aura that glowed around him.

Death.

That demon was walking death, and if his aura so much as touched you, that was it. Finito. Done.

Even worse—he *liked* it. The aura wasn't a defense mechanism. When the Deavalus demon got to earth, he ran around killing mindlessly and cackling with joy as he did so.

Or so I'd heard.

His kind had been a myth to me until now.

Myth no longer.

Yeah, I preferred enchanted animals and ancient gods in my myths.

Would his magic even work in the prison? Or was he so strong that the dampening spell here couldn't repress his power entirely?

Yeah, I didn't want to find out.

I kept going, my footsteps silent as I passed demons, mages, and vampires.

Some twitched as I passed, looking toward the hall with curious expressions.

I was nearly to the end when the voice came.

"I can smell you."

I stiffened, heart pounding.

"You're close, newcomer."

A shiver raced over my skin as I turned to see where the voice was coming from.

To my left, a demon stood at the door of his cage. He was tall and slender, with skin the color of burnt orange and fiery red eyes. His horns were short and sawed off.

"Why don't you open this door?" he hissed.

Yeah, no.

I turned away to keep walking, but movement flashed out of

the corner of my eye. I flinched, instinct propelling me away, but the demon managed to grab me.

My heart leapt into my throat as he slammed me against his cell bars.

He'd stretched his arms out six feet!

How the hell had he done that?"

"Nullifier!" His whispered voice sounded delighted.

Oh, shit.

My power must've been reacting in some weird way here, disengaging the protection charms or something. For whatever reason, my nullifying magic worked even though the rest of my magic didn't.

Mega shit.

I yanked hard on his arm, nearly tearing it off so I could dart away. The demon yowled, then reached for me with another freakishly long limb. Claws glinted in the electric light as they neared my face.

I swatted his arm away, panting.

But it was too late. The other demons had started shouting, pounding at their cell doors. Declan entered a half second later, his panicked gaze searching for me.

The guards showed up a moment later.

Damn, they're fast.

And prepared.

They hit Declan with a potion bomb as soon as he'd drawn a sword from the ether. I darted to the wall, pressing myself up against it and hoping no one could see me or hear me. I drew my sword, ready to fight my way out of this if necessary.

The damned demon with the long arms pointed right at me. "The ghost is there!"

I wasn't about to correct the moron that I wasn't a ghost.

Two of the guards—burly mages wearing all black—turned

toward me. One wore a strange metal band around his big head, and he tapped it.

As soon as he did, his eyes zeroed right in on me.

Shit.

That damned headband was something that allowed him to see through invisibility—I'd bet my car on it.

I raised my hands. "We're just here for information."

He didn't bother responding. Or if he did, I didn't hear him. Something hit me from the side, and I collapsed on the ground, unconscious.

Pain thundered in my head. I groaned, rolling over on the hard floor and nearly vomiting.

Normally, when I woke, there was a slight moment of confusion if I wasn't in my own bed.

Not now.

At this moment, it was clear that I was *screwed.*

I opened my eyes and blinked, my vision clearing to reveal a barren stone floor that led to stone wall.

Prison.

Aching, I dragged myself upright. Declan lay on the ground next to me, unconscious. I scrambled over to him and shook his shoulders.

"Declan!" I whispered, frantic. "Come on. Be okay! Get up!"

There was nothing, and for the briefest, most horrible moment, I thought he might be dead. Something inside me tore at the thought, and it hurt. Physically hurt.

I pressed a hand to my chest to still the ache and leaned over him. "Come on. Get up."

He didn't move.

My heart felt like it was tearing out of my chest.

Was this it? Would I lose Declan to a potion bomb I hadn't even seen coming?

No.

I refused to accept it.

Just as I refused to accept that we were trapped in a stone box in the most secure, dangerous prison in the world.

This was not how I wanted to go out.

I'd lived my whole life as wary as a feral cat. True, I had my reasons. Those I'd trusted—both my family and my first real friend in the outside world—had betrayed Mari and me. Betrayed us to the point that we'd ended up captives. Tools for evil.

And we'd retreated. Not truly trusting anyone—not with our whole hearts—for fear that it could happen again.

Well, this was the worst that could happen. Trapped in a stone box with Declan possibly dead. And I'd spent the whole time I'd known him pushing him away.

I'd even used the nullification to push him away.

I should have tried to make it work with Declan—whatever it was. A relationship? Just getting to know him?

Hell, anything.

I shook him again, tears prickling my eyes.

His chest moved on a breath, and my shoulders sagged.

Thank fates.

The guards had been able to see him—how big and strong he was—so no doubt they'd dosed him with extra knock-out juice. And whatever it was made of, it was strong.

Heart thundering, I reached into the ether and withdrew the potion bag that I'd stashed there. I sorted through it, finally finding an energy potion.

This had better work.

I pinched his jaw and dragged it open, then poured the

liquid down his throat. He swallowed and sputtered, finally sitting up.

I threw my arms around him. "Thank fates you're all right."

He coughed and pulled back, searching my face. "Are you okay? You looked devastated."

I wiped a few tears from my face and ignored the question. "How are you?"

"Alive." He rubbed his forehead, clearly trying to remember. "We were caught?"

"Yeah. The prisoners started a ruckus and the guards found us. Hit us with all they had, too."

He dragged his hand down his face. "Clearly."

Confident that he was all right, I turned from him, inspecting the room. It was a small box of a space—ten feet by ten feet—with no window and just a metal door.

"They're taking no chances with us," I said.

"You'd think they'd ask why we're here."

"I tried to tell them we just wanted info." I shrugged. "Then they slammed me with the knock-out juice."

"They'll come back to interrogate us."

I swallowed hard. I probably wouldn't enjoy interrogation. "Then let's get the hell out of here."

I stood, grabbing my potion bag, and went to the door. Carefully, I inspected it. The big lock was a sturdy mechanism. I patted my pockets, unsurprised to find them empty. They'd taken the keys I'd stolen from the guard.

I raised my bag of potions, grinning. They hadn't thought to check the ether.

"Have you got something in there to get us out of here?" Declan asked, his voice low.

"I should." I rummaged around in the bag and pulled out a cobalt blue bottle of potion. "This will melt just about anything."

Declan eyed the lock, then drew his sword from the ether and spoke, his voice barely audible. "There will be a guard on the other side. I'd bet my best whiskey on it."

I nodded and uncapped the little bottle, then dripped it onto the lock. My breath caught in my throat as I watched. Waited.

Come on.

I poured some more, trying to splash it into the lock. The metal began to fizz, the potion eating away at it.

"It's working," Declan murmured as the metal was destroyed.

I stepped back, drawing my mace from the ether. Whatever was on the other side, I wanted to be ready.

Finally, the lock disappeared. The door swung open, dragged by its own weight.

Declan lunged out into the hall.

I followed.

There was one guard, a burly man who stood next to the door. He jumped when Declan appeared next to him, but moved too slow. Declan had his arm around the guard's throat in a flash. He pulled tight, cutting off the guard's air until he passed out.

"No point in killing him," he said, stashing his sword in the ether. "Stand guard."

I did as he asked, turning to inspect the hall as Declan bound the guard in his own cuffs and gagged him.

The hall was empty save for our cell—clearly a holding area for dangerous, unknown prisoners.

They hadn't realized how dangerous we really were, thank fates.

Declan dragged the body into the cell, then returned.

I met his gaze. "We still have no idea where Cell Block Z is."

Wally appeared at my feet, the shadow sprite at his side. Both of the small, smoky figures looked up at me.

"Great timing." I grinned at Wally. "Can you ask your friend where Cell Block Z is?"

Wally looked at the shadow sprite, who seemed to vibrate with nervous energy. He bounced on skinny legs, barely reaching my knees.

After a while, Wally looked back at me. *Follow us.*

I shot Declan a grin. He nodded back.

Wally set off down the hall, following the shadow sprite. The little figure floated more than he walked, and he moved quickly. I had to trot to keep up.

Wally turned back to look at me. *We're taking the back way.*

"Perfect." I looked at Declan and translated, since he couldn't hear Wally.

The shadow sprite led us through narrow corridors that seemed to be built into the walls, almost. At points, I had to turn sideways to fit through, and Declan got stuck a couple times.

Finally, we reached a hallway that was lit only by a couple of old light bulbs that flickered weakly, revealing an ancient hall lined with empty cells.

"This is it." I didn't ask it as a question. It was too obvious.

This was the oldest part of the prison, no longer in use. There wasn't any electric light, and some of the cells were missing their doors.

Even better, the dampening spell that had repressed my magic in the active part of the prison wasn't working here. I could feel the power flowing through my veins again, thank fates. Not just the nullifying power, but all of my magic.

"We're looking for the cell of Acius the fallen angel."

The shadow sprite turned and walked down the hall. We followed. With every footstep, my heartbeat ratcheted up.

This was it.

This was where we would find our answers.

The spirit led us into a dark little cell, and I shined my light on the interior.

There was nothing.

Not even scratches on the wall to count down the days.

What the hell?

"There's nothing here." My devastation sounded in my voice.

"We don't know that yet." Declan went to the walls and began to search, feeling around each stone block.

Wally helped, sniffing at the corners of the room. The sprite just stood there, seeming frightened.

I blinked at him. He'd been anxious before, but now he was downright scared. Why? We were just in an empty cell. This should be the least dangerous place.

I knelt to look at him, realizing that it felt colder near the ground. Ghost cold, almost. There was a sparkling energy, too. Not quite malevolent, but definitely unpleasant.

Was there something here, after all? Something we couldn't see?

I closed my eyes and tried to get a feel for it. What was it?

I couldn't figure it out, so I looked at Wally. "Can you ask your friend if there are ghosts here? Or spirits of some kind?"

Wally turned to look at me, his red eyes blazing, then strolled toward the sprite. The two communicated, silent as usual, while I waited, drumming my fingertips on the ground.

Declan kept searching the stone walls.

Finally, Wally looked at me. *There is a ghost here. A woman.*

"Can he speak to her?"

There was a moment while they conferred, then Wally looked at me and shook his head.

"Does she know about Acius?"

After a moment, Wally spoke. *She was here the same time as him.*

That was it, then. She was our clue.

Except, we couldn't speak to her. Unless...

I looked at Declan. "You're an angel. Can you speak to the dead?"

He turned from where he was poking into a hole in the wall and met my gaze. "Unfortunately, no. Not on earth, at least."

Shit.

I sat back on my butt.

How the hell did anyone survive in this awful place?

They went crazy. It was the only explanation. If Acius hadn't been crazy before he'd gotten here—which, who was I kidding, he'd probably been crazy—he was nuts by the time he left.

The cold seeped into me, along with the feeling of being watched.

The ghost.

I needed to talk to her.

She was our only clue. My only way to figure out where Mari was.

Talking to ghosts wasn't a skill I currently had, but I *could* have it. If I wanted it badly enough.

Quickly, I sliced my thumbnail across my finger. A spark of pain was followed by a drop of blood. I used my dragon magic, envisioning myself contacting the ghost.

At first, there was nothing.

I closed my eyes and tried harder, calling upon the magic in my soul to create a new power. At least temporarily. I just needed to speak to her for a moment.

I could feel the magical energy in the air increase. It felt as if there was another presence here.

Yes!

I was getting close. I could almost feel her. The chill of her presence on the left side of the room. She was watching me.

I opened my eyes, looking for her.

There was no one there.

But I could *feel* her.

I tried harder, pulling on all of the magic in my soul. Though I could feel the ghost's presence still, it wasn't enough to actually summon her. To talk to her.

My shoulders sagged.

Shit.

I'd been afraid of this.

I wasn't using enough blood. With my Dragon Blood ability to create magical skills, more blood equaled stronger magic.

Contacting this ghost required more powerful magic, which required more blood.

The downside, though...

It could make this skill permanent. Yet another permanent magic, changing my signature forever.

It was a risk.

I drew in a shuddery breath. There was only one thing I could do.

Open my veins and create new magic.

13

I raised my gaze to Declan.

I didn't want to do this in front of him, but there was no choice. It was the only way to get the information I needed to save Mari.

And I'd do anything for her.

I'd already decided to try to trust him. What was the point of my epiphany back in that cell if I couldn't trust him with this? It was part of me.

"I'm going to create new magic," I said. "We need to talk to this ghost, and it's the only way."

"Permanent magic?"

"Yes. I've tried to create temporary magic." I held up my bleeding finger. "It wasn't enough. Ghosts are tricky. They straddle the line between life and death, and I need more power to contact her."

"It would be enough power that the magic could become permanent, then?"

"Yes." That was what changed my magical signature, what made it more obvious to the world that *I* was changed. Different. Dangerous.

Would this be the time that I made too much magic? Would it increase my magical signature to the point that I couldn't hide it anymore?

Fates, I hoped not.

"Considering that the alternative is you dying from the curse or us never finding your sister, I'd say it's worth the risk."

I nodded, glad that he'd agreed so easily. That he acted like it was the most normal thing in the world. I didn't want to do this, but if I had to, I appreciated the support.

Carefully, I shifted into position, kneeling on the hard stone ground. I sliced my sharp thumbnail across both of my arms. Pain shot through me as blood pooled on my skin.

I tilted my arms to the ground so it could pour onto the stone.

It hurt, but fear didn't fill me. Not like it had when I'd done this last week.

It almost felt like the process was getting easier.

That alone should make me nervous, but I was so full of worry for Mari that there was no room left in me for other concerns.

I looked away from Declan as my head began to grow woozy. My blood flowed out of me, weakening me with every second that passed. Once enough had spilled onto the stone, I pushed out my magic as well, giving everything I had.

As I worked, I envisioned exactly what I wanted: to be able to see this ghost and speak to her. To ask her where Acius was.

I swayed where I sat. Declan came to his knees next to me, and I could feel his concerned gaze on my face. It warmed me, but I ignored it, focusing instead on the magic that I wanted to create.

My desire to speak to the ghost roared through me.

I have to do this.

I have to finish.

"Isn't this enough?" Declan asked.

"No." Blackness started to steal in at the corners of my vision.

Creating new magic required sacrifice. In my case, I had to almost die. Maybe one day, while trying this, I actually *would* die.

My breathing grew shallow as I worked, draining my blood onto the stones and forcing my magic out with it. My heartbeat raced and my skin chilled. Wally joined me, brushing his smoky fur against my side, giving me some of his strength. It wasn't enough to keep me going, though. But then, that was the point. I was about to collapse when the magic in the air changed.

Finally.

It sparked with energy, swirling and bright, then flowed back into me, surging into my soul and lighting me up from within.

I gasped and straightened, power rushing through me. My eyes popped open as my veins filled with fresh blood. Strength rushed into my muscles, making me feel like I could pick up a truck.

I sucked in a breath and focused on the new magic that I'd created. It felt chilly inside of me—a bit like the ghost.

I leaned back, away from the puddle of my blood, and looked around the room.

"You can show yourself," I said.

There was nothing there.

So I called upon my new power, drawing out the cold magic and letting it fill the air. Like a welcoming committee for the one I wanted to speak to.

"Are you all right?" Declan asked. Gently, he gripped my arm, and I looked at him.

"I'm fine. Really." I turned back to the other side of the room, to where I thought the ghost stood. "Come out. We just have some questions."

Magic fizzed in the air, as if she had heard me and

responded. Wally and the shadow sprite watched anxiously, interest gleaming in their eyes.

I poured more of my new magic into the room, determined to talk to this damned ghost. After what I'd just done, there was no way I was walking out of here without the info we'd come for.

Finally, the ghost appeared.

She was a tall woman, skinny and hard-looking. Her dress was ragged and her hair dirty. The look in her dark eyes was slightly crazed, and now that I could see her, I could also feel her signature.

Yuck.

She smelled of a dumpster and felt like slime.

This woman was evil.

And maybe crazy.

Her dark eyes flicked down to the white blood on the floor. "What are you? What did you do?"

Her words were slightly garbled, but I could understand her.

"I created new magic."

She gasped. "Not possible."

Her words still sounded a bit strange, and I realized that she was probably speaking another language. But I could still understand her. My ghost power, translating perhaps?

I shrugged and turned on my iciest voice. "I'm powerful, what can I say?"

She cooed her interest and drifted forward. "Impressive."

Okay, good. I had some cred with the crazy, evil ghost. Probably because she thought Dragon Bloods were evil. Some of us were, especially those who'd been driven mad by power.

"Why are you here?" she asked. She chilled the air around me, and I shivered.

"We're looking for Acius."

Her eyes took on a dreamy cast. Yep, she *definitely* recognized him. And if I wasn't wrong, she totally had the hots for him, too.

Ew.

I could dive right into questions about him, but I didn't want to scare her off. Just because I had the ability to talk to her didn't mean that I could *force* her to talk.

"Who are you?" I asked. "You don't look like the type to be in a prison like this."

She kind of did, actually. But people loved to prove other people wrong.

"Oh, but appearances are deceiving." She cackled, the sound icing the blood in my veins. Her ragged hair quivered around her head, and her eyes took on an intense light. "I'm responsible for the genocide of 1252. In Wallachia."

I searched my mind for a memory of it, but came up with nothing. Either way, genocide was enough for anyone to end up in this place.

Clearly, she was proud of her accomplishments.

I swallowed the bile in my throat and tried to sound impressed. "Well done. That was quite the spectacle."

Her eyes brightened. "You've heard of it?"

I nodded. "Oh, yes. I've admired your work for a long time."

She leaned forward. "What was your favorite part?"

Ah, shit. I'd gone too far.

The heads. Wally's voice drifted to me. The ghost didn't startle or look toward him, so I assumed she couldn't hear him. *Say, "The heads."*

"The heads." I nodded like I was really into what I was saying. "Definitely the heads. Really...cool."

Cool? Probably the wrong word, but this was freaking tough.

"I know, they were wonderful." She looked into the distance, a dreamy expression on her face.

All right, this woman was a nut. An evil nut.

"And you met Acius here," I said, trying to push her into talking more now that she was in a good mood.

"Oh, I did." She leaned back against the wall, as if we were about to have a gab session. Her form drifted slightly through the stone, but she stopped herself from disappearing. "I was already here. He arrived shortly after. He'd broken ties with the High Court of the Angels in the *worst* way possible." She giggled and met my eyes. "He killed twelve other angels!"

Shit. He was strong, if he could do that. And evil, considering the angels were a tight bunch, from what I'd heard.

"Wow, so impressive." I tried to make my voice sound awed and didn't look at Declan. This was fucked up, but she clearly liked the guy so much she'd talk about his *accomplishments* all day long.

"Wasn't it? And those first years here were...wonderful."

I worked to hide my grimace. "Until he escaped, of course."

"Oh yes. We planned it for ages."

"You went with him?"

She nodded excitedly, but only for a moment. Then her face fell. "I died in the attempt." She tilted her head, confusion flashing across her face. "Or did he kill me?"

Disappointment surged from the ghost, so strong I could feel it.

Shit, this was going the wrong direction. If she was bummed, she might disappear.

I held out my hands in a placating gesture, determined to distract her. To get her back on track. "Don't worry about that right now. I'm sure he didn't. Tell me, where did he go?"

She smiled, excited again. "Well, I was able to follow him, you see. On account of our strong bond."

Yes. Hell yes. This was exactly what I was looking for.

"He's worth following," I said, nearly gagging on the words.

"Oh, he is."

I nodded encouragingly.

"He wandered for a while, committing *all* kinds of atrocities."

She couldn't have sounded more admiring if she tried, and I wanted to punch her. Fates, she was a piece of work. "But finally, he settled on a place in Grimrealm."

Yes.

"I'm from Grimrealm!" I said, trying to sound excited. "That's so amazing."

She nodded, then tilted her head. "Wait. You don't want him for your own, do you?"

"Oh no." I pointed to Declan. "That's my man, there. He's not as evil as Acius." I shook my head as if disappointed. "But he's working on it."

Declan nodded, but wisely kept his mouth shut.

"Oh, good." The ghost visibly relaxed. "Well, he created the cleverest place to live. Right off the cemetery. So secret that you can't even find the little door that leads to it."

A little door in the cemetery. Holy shit, this was something. This was a *real* clue.

For the briefest moment, fear flared. Was my family somehow involved in this? If he was in Grimrealm, it was possible.

But unlikely. We'd never had anything to do with the cemetery, and my aunt and uncle had been small-time criminals. The fallen angel was the boss in this scenario, so they certainly weren't controlling him.

Thank fates, because we had enough to deal with in terms of Acius. I didn't need any kind of shitty family reunion.

"Someone's coming." Declan's voice broke in through my excitement.

I jerked, looking up at him. "What?"

"A guard, someone. I don't know who, but I can hear them."

I could hear them, too, now that I was paying attention.

The ghost disappeared, just winking out of existence. I could feel her absence keenly. The air warmed and the sickly feeling in my stomach dissipated.

I surged to my feet, stumbling back from the puddle of my white blood. The guards wouldn't be able to recognize it, but even so...

"Let's get the hell out of here." I looked at Wally. "Can your friend lead us out?"

Wally nodded. *I can. I've seen the whole place. Come on.*

He hurried to the entryway, and we followed.

As soon as I stepped out into the hallway, I spotted the guards. There were three of them, all at least six feet tall and armed to the teeth with magic. Their signatures surged toward us, fiercely strong.

Wally veered to go down the hall in the other direction.

"Hey!" The lead guard shouted after us, but we ignored him.

I sprinted down the hall after Wally and the sprite, Declan at my side. A quick glance back revealed that the guards had fired up their power. Blue light glowed around the hand of the guard in the front, and he hurled it at us.

"Sonic boom!" I shouted.

Declan and I darted out of the way, and the boom plowed into the ground in front of us, nearly hitting Wally.

I turned around and shouted, "Asshole! He's just a cat!"

"That's no cat," the guard growled.

Declan turned and hurled a blast of heavenly fire at the guards. It hit the one on the right, who went down hard. The fireball that he'd been about to throw at us fizzled out.

The lead guard threw another sonic boom.

This one was so big that it filled the whole corridor.

"Shield!" I drew mine from the ether, and Declan followed suit.

We turned to face the blue blast of light, raising our shields just in time. The sonic boom plowed into us, throwing us backward. Pain shot through my arms, but I managed to stay on my feet. Declan did, as well.

As soon as the force dissipated, we turned and ran, sprinting out of the hall and down the corridor to the right.

"Closest exit, Wally," I shouted. "Don't care where it is."

Wally sprinted ahead, and I thanked fates for him.

Declan fired off two blasts of heavenly fire at the guards who were only twenty feet behind us. I looked back to see them both go down in a burst of flame.

"Are they dead?" I asked. I'd kill some guards to save my sister, no problem. But not if I didn't have to. These guys were just doing their jobs, after all.

"No," Declan said. "But they won't be happy."

"Fine with me."

Wally led us into a big room that was full of guards. At least six of them, all sitting at a table and playing a card game.

Shit.

Just our luck.

It was empty earlier! Wally charged one of the guards, leaping onto him and breathing a blast of fire into his face. The little sprite disappeared, and I couldn't blame him.

Declan drew his sword from the ether and charged, his shield raised to block any oncoming magic. I called upon my mace, grateful for the comforting weight in my hand.

A guard to the left—a tall one with the glowing blue eyes of some kind of ice mage—hurled an icicle at me. I dodged left, and the ice grazed my thigh.

I swung my mace and charged, hitting him in the side. Not enough to kill, but enough to incapacitate. He slammed to the ground.

Declan took out two mages with his sword, all while dodging fireballs. Wally leapt onto another, breathing fire right in his face. The guard shrieked and staggered backward, trying to get away. I went for the last guard, swinging my mace for his side.

He dodged it and slid under the table.

"Coward," I shouted.

He scowled and hurled a blast of fire at me. I dived right, but I was too slow. The flame plowed into my shin, and I went down hard. I rolled on my leg, dampening the fire, then surged upright.

Pissed, I drew a dagger from the ether and hurled it at the mage, hitting him in the thigh.

All around me, there was chaos. Guards on the ground, shouting. Wally looking like he was waiting for someone to die so he could eat their soul.

An alarm sounded, blaring through the compound.

"More guards coming," Declan said.

"Let's get the hell out of here." I looked at Wally. "Lead the way."

Wally raced from the room, and I followed, limping on my burned leg. Pain shot through me with every step, but I ignored it, pushing forward and racing after my hellcat.

He led us to the exterior of the castle, high on the cliffs over the sea. We were nowhere near the boat.

I sprinted to the edge of the cliff and looked down into the water. "Looks deep, right?"

"It's dark enough to fly," Declan said.

I looked up. He was right. The clouds had covered the moon.

Shouts sounded from behind us. I looked back. More guards spilled out of the gate.

Shit.

I moved toward Declan. "Let's go."

His wings flared behind his back, and he picked me up, launching us into the sky. The guards shouted from below.

I called on my shield, leaning over to hold it in a way that blocked the worst of the guard's fireballs. Soon, we were far enough away that they couldn't reach us.

With the threat gone—mostly—I looked at Declan. He was pale, and it probably wasn't from any of his wounds.

Immediately, I called upon my nullifying magic, trying to shove it deep down inside myself.

Declan's brow relaxed. "Thanks."

I just nodded, not willing to acknowledge the step I'd taken. I was working on controlling my magic.

So we can be together.

Yeah, now wasn't exactly the time.

We needed to get the hell out of here and save my sister. Save my life. Just the thought of it reminded me of the fire burning through my veins. I was able to forget about it, at least a little bit, while in the heat of battle.

But when I wasn't fighting, I could feel it inside me, growing ever stronger. I was running out of time.

We needed to get home.

I called on the bag of potions I'd stashed in the ether. It appeared in my hand, and Declan looked down at it.

"You got a transport charm in there?" he asked. "Because the guards searched my pockets and took mine."

"Indeed I do." I pulled it out and held it up. "I'll toss it in the air."

If it didn't hit ground and shatter, it would ignite in the air a couple seconds after being thrown. He nodded, and I tossed it. The charm exploded into a cloud of silvery gray dust, and Declan flew into it.

The ether sucked us up and spun us around, sending us back to Magic's Bend.

14

THE ETHER SPAT US OUT IN FRONT OF POTIONS & PASTILLES, THE coffee shop near the FireSouls shop and home. The street in Factory Row was quiet at this late afternoon hour, but I spotted Connor inside his shop.

"Come on." I strode toward the shop, and Declan followed.

"Hang on." Declan grabbed my arm, and I stopped. "You're limping. Badly."

My leg ached, as if it'd only needed to be reminded.

"Let me heal you."

Before I could respond, he was using his heavenly light to heal my wound. Warmth surged through me, followed by relief.

I met his eyes. "Thanks."

He nodded, and I couldn't help but think that he took better care of me than I did.

As I walked, I dug into my pocket and pulled out my cell phone, then dialed Nix. She picked up on the first ring.

"Any luck?" she asked.

"Yeah, I've got a lead. Where are you?"

"Just returned from Grimrealm. We struck out again."

"Well, we're about to go back. Meet us at Potions & Pastilles."

"Be there in five."

I opened the door to the coffee shop and walked in. It was empty save for Connor, who was behind the counter, wearing one of his usual band T-Shirts. The scrawling writing said P!nk.

He looked up, his floppy dark hair a mess and his face pale. "Did you find them?"

"Not yet." I joined him. "But we have a good lead, and we're going back to Grimrealm. They're there."

"Need backup?"

I smiled. "Yeah, that'd be helpful."

He nodded, then hiked a thumb toward the back of the cafe, where I knew he kept his potions workshop. "I'll pack up."

"Cool. Do you have any kind of pep-up potion? I think Mordaca's going to need it when we find her." If she hadn't had a chance to take the second dose of the antidote that delayed the curse, she'd be feeling like shit. Since we might have to fight our way to get to the cure—*please, fates, let Acius have the cure on him*--she'd need to be as strong as possible.

He nodded. "Sure, I can grab something."

"Thanks. The others will be here soon. Then we'll plan."

He nodded. "I'll be quick. Help yourself to anything in the case. You must be starved."

As Connor disappeared through the swinging door toward the back, I ducked behind the counter to grab a couple of the Cornish pasties. Connor and Claire had come over from southwest England years ago, and they'd brought the distinctly British delicacy with them.

"Have a preference?" I asked Declan, nodding down at the pastries, which were basically meat and veggie pies shaped like half-moons.

"No, anything is fine."

I grabbed three and handed him two, then got a couple glasses of water. We sat at the biggest table in the place and ate quickly. I had absolutely no appetite—to the point that even the savory beef and potato filling did nothing for me—but I felt stronger as I ate.

I kept my eyes glued to the door, like a kid on Christmas Eve, waiting for Santa to land on the roof. Except grim determination filled me instead of excitement.

I'd just popped the last bite of pastry in my mouth when Roarke, Cass, Nix, and Claire walked in. Roarke was Del's boyfriend, and they all looked exhausted, with shadows under their eyes and pale skin. Worse, they reeked of Grimrealm.

They strode toward us and sat heavily in the chairs across the table. Connor joined us a half second later, hurrying up and dropping into a seat next to his sister.

Roarke leaned forward, concern in his dark eyes. He was half demon, and Warden of the Underworld, and I swore the stress of this was starting to make his inner demon come out. He was one of the good ones, though. The *only* good one, actually. The only one of his type.

"What did you find?" he asked, voice gravelly with worry.

I told them about the graveyard and the hidden door, and the three of them frowned.

"We were in the graveyard hours ago," Nix said, a frown creasing her pale face. She crossed her arms over the T-shirt she wore, covering up the cartoon cat that rode a rainbow Pop-Tart. I didn't understand the reference, but I rarely did. "There was nothing that we could find."

"The concealment charm on that angel is strong," Cass said thoughtfully. "We were looking for him—or for Mordaca or Del. We *weren't* looking for a hidden door."

Nix nodded, considering. "Okay. So we go back and look for this door."

"And kick some ass." Claire scowled. "I can't take the stress anymore."

Roarke dragged a hand over his face, weary and worried. "Good work, Aerdeca. I can't thank you enough."

His stress and fear tugged at something in me. We were all united in this. The fear cloaked all of us, like a horrible bond. For the briefest second, I wanted to tell them to call me Aeri. I'd been hiding too long.

But now wasn't the time.

"We'll get them back." I stood. "Everyone grab a bite or replenish your weapons. We'll head out of here in ten." I looked between Cass and Nix. "I think this is it. Final fight. Now's the time to call Aidan and Ares if they're available."

Aidan and Ares were their partners, respectively. Both were immensely powerful and useful in a fight.

Cass nodded. "I'll get them. They'll want to be there to help."

They all stood, each looking tired but determined. As they scattered, I turned to Declan. I could see the understanding in his eyes. He got how hard this was. How the worry was about to crush me. I hadn't heard from Mari since she'd first been abducted. Anything could have happened to her.

I drew in a shuddery breath.

He pulled me to him, and I collapsed into his arms, letting him hug me. I hugged him back, absorbing some of his strength and comfort.

"We'll get them back," he said.

"I know." We had to. I couldn't live with anything different.

Twenty minutes later, we stood at the start of Fairlight Alley, the entrance to Grimrealm. Cass, Nix, Connor, Claire, Declan and I all wore a cloak to conceal our identities, along with a charm around our necks that gave us a dark magic signature. Going in with just my own enhanced dark magic had bitten me in the ass last time, and I couldn't afford any more distractions.

Hopefully, this would allow us to blend with the inhabitants of Grimrealm without being noticed.

Cass looked at her watch, then up at me. "They'll be here any minute."

As if they'd heard her speak, two tall men turned and walked around the corner. They were both well over six feet with broad shoulders and a long gait.

Aidan, Cass's guy, was The Origin, a descendant of the original Shifter. As such, he was the most powerful of his kind, able to transform into any animal at all. He preferred the griffin for fighting. Ares, who was with Nix, was a vampire. He was one of the most powerful in existence, one of the three members of the Vampire Court, the ruling body of vampires.

They'd apparently been off dealing with a dangerous artifact from the FireSouls' shop to give the women the freedom to look for Del and Mari.

"Sorry that took so long." Aidan stopped in front of us.

"You're fine." Cass handed each of them a cloak and a charm to conceal themselves, then turned to me. "Let's go."

I sucked in a deep breath and nodded, then turned to face the alley. I was visiting Grimrealm with unsettling frequency these days.

In record time, we made our way down the alley and through the trapdoor that was set into the ground at the end. When we dropped into the underground tunnel, it looked as usual, with the green torches flaming bright.

There was no one around, thank fates, and we strode toward the main part of Grimrealm, easily able to avoid the protective charms now that we knew what they were. I just fed my nullification magic into the wall, and we avoided the slower moving ice.

Damn, this power was handy.

When we reached the end of the tunnel, we stopped at the true entrance to Grimrealm. It made me nervous every time. I hated that, since I was rarely nervous in real life.

Grimrealm wasn't real life though. It was a nightmare past, one I wanted to put to rest eventually.

I stared out at the market that was situated under the huge dome with hundreds of black tents and even more people bustling between them. As usual, the signs floated in the air above the tents, advertising everything from potions to food to weapons and other horrible things I didn't want to think about.

The stench of dark magic rolled over me, making me shiver.

"I can lead us to the graveyard," Nix said.

"Thanks." I actually had no idea how to get there. I'd never visited as a child.

I stuck close to Declan as Nix led us through the market. It hummed with activity, and I passed tables covered with shrunken heads—real—and diamonds—probably not real. There was everything in between, but I kept my eyes on the people around me instead of on the goods. I didn't want to run into any trouble before we got to Mari and Del.

My shoulders relaxed slightly as we departed the market. Nix led us to one of the many huge tunnels that led off the main market square. They were like roads in the underground Grimrealm, leading to other neighborhoods and districts, most of which I'd never visited.

This one was mostly empty, with just a few souls passing back and forth. There were no doors or shops in this tunnel, just barren stone walls.

By the time we made it to the graveyard, I was buzzing with nerves.

At the sight of the view, Connor whistled low under his breath. "Whew, that's something."

As I took in the view, I couldn't help but agree. The graveyard was at least the size of the market, but instead of activity, there was silence. Thousands of gravestones and mausoleums filled the space. Somehow, mist managed to crawl over the ground, though I had no idea where it was coming from.

I turned to Cass and Nix. "Can you feel anything?"

"Give me a moment," Cass murmured.

Nix already had her eyes closed, clearly trying to focus on her magic and her surroundings. This time, instead of using their dragon magic to look for Mari and Del, they were looking for a hidden door.

I hoped it made a difference.

Tension crawled across my skin as I waited. We *could* physically search for the door—and I would, if they couldn't lead us to it—but we didn't have a lot of time to spare. Even now, the fire in my veins burned. It weakened my muscles, no matter how hard I tried to ignore it. That didn't bode well for me *or* Mari.

Finally, Nix's head popped up. "I've got something."

"Me too." Cass pointed ahead and slightly to the right. "That way."

My heart thundered as we hurried across the cemetery, weaving between the gravestones and mausoleums. Cold mist twisted around my ankles, making me shiver.

Wally appeared at my side, trotting through the mist. *Nice place.*

"Your judgment is skewed," I said.

He looked up at me, then shook his head in disgust. *You don't know how to appreciate the finer things.*

Despite the worry that twisted my insides, the smallest smile tugged at my lips.

Cass stopped abruptly. "Here. It's around here."

I halted, searching the area around us. We'd reached a spot where there were three small mausoleums. None of them had a visible door—it was as if they'd been all bricked up. The ground underfoot was trampled a bit more in this area, but it didn't point to one building over another. I walked around the little structures, searching for a door.

When I finished my circuit, I looked at Nix and Cass. "There's no door."

"No door that we can *see*."

I nodded. "Secret door. Of course."

"How do we reveal it?" Declan asked.

"I've got something for that." Connor stepped forward, digging into his potion bag.

I stepped back, giving him space to work.

He looked at Nix and Cass. "Any idea which one it might be?"

They frowned and walked in a circle around the three mausoleums.

Cass met Connor's eyes. "Could be any one of them."

He nodded. "Well, I've only got enough potion for two, so cross your fingers. If we're lucky, it will reveal the door hidden behind the spell."

I watched, breath held, as he splashed some of his potion on the first building. Nothing happened.

Damn.

He moved toward the other two, looking between them. Then he pointed, silently mouthing some words that looked a lot like *eeny, meeny, miney, mo.* Finally, he settled on one.

I squeezed Declan's hand as I watched him splash the rest of the potion on the mausoleum to the right.

Tension thrummed in the air as we watched, until finally, magic sparked around the little building. Slowly, a door began to appear.

Yes! "Thank you, Connor."

He grinned. "Just glad it worked."

I approached the door and hovered my hand over the handle. Dark magic pricked against me, reaching right into my soul and punching hard.

I stepped back. "Death."

"Death?" Declan frowned at me.

"If you touch it without permission, you're dead." But I had my nullifying magic. I reached for the door again.

Declan grabbed my hand. "No."

I looked at him. "Yes. I have to."

"Even with your nullifying magic, it's too dangerous." Worry tightened his mouth.

I looked around. "Anyone else have any ideas?"

Worry flashed on every single person's face, eyes darkening and brows creasing. But no one said anything.

"Well, that settles it." I looked at Declan. "It's my *sister*. I don't really have a choice. And I don't think I'm going to die."

It'd probably hurt like hell, though. No way I was getting out of this unscathed.

Finally, Declan released my arm, but he didn't look happy about it.

I gave him a long look, then reached for the door. I called upon my nullifying magic before I even touched it, trying to force it out of myself to get a head start. The power swelled within me, making me vaguely ill with its strength. I grabbed the door handle and yanked.

Electric pain shot up my arm. I gritted my teeth as tears pricked at my eyes. Once the door was open, I gestured to my friends, who hurried through.

Declan waited until last, and as soon as he'd gone, I followed, letting go of the door handle as quickly as I could.

Darkness enveloped me within the mausoleum. Stale air filled the room, and I breathed shallowly, feeling my way toward the stairs that led downward. I followed Declan, joining the trail of my friends as we descended farther into the earth. After about fifty steps, the path leveled out.

The tunnel was creepy and narrow, with rough rock walls and no light.

"Forest up ahead," a whispered voice filtered back.

It was a game of telephone, one person passing the news to the person behind them.

When I stepped out of the tunnel and joined my friends, I doused the light of my ring. We stood in a large clearing in the woods, surrounded by a ring of trees. A pale light emitted from the top of the cavern above us. The rock ceiling was so high overhead that it was like being in perpetual twilight, and already, I felt claustrophobic.

Was this a natural cavern in the earth, or something magic-made?

"Trees underground?" Connor asked.

I approached one to my right, touching the blackened bark. "I'm not sure they're alive."

"There's a path up ahead." Declan pointed to the worn place between the trees, about fifty yards away. We just had to cross the clearing to get to it.

I looked at Nix and Cass. "Do you guys feel anything?"

They both frowned.

"I can't sense them, no," Nix said. "It feels the same as it did back in Grimrealm."

Declan studied the clearing. "That's a powerful concealment charm."

"Let's follow the path, then."

The nine of us set off across the clearing. Though we were technically underground, it didn't feel like that. It felt like walking through a haunted forest at dusk.

We were nearly to the path when several of the skeletal trees shifted.

I stiffened, eying them warily.

Four of them moved toward us, gray magic swirling around their forms. Their limbs and bark transformed, turning them into skeletal demons with long limbs tipped with white claws. Each had two legs—sort of—and two arms. The heads were just long pillars of jagged wood. No eyes, noses, or mouths.

I'd never seen anything like them. But the dark magic that swelled from them made it clear—they were here to hurt us.

"They don't look sentient," Cass said.

She was right. They looked more like magic than a living thing. "But they do look deadly."

The four creatures charged us, claws raised. Each one was at least twelve feet tall.

My heart thundered as their footsteps shook the ground.

I drew my mace from the ether and sprinted forward. The metal was a comforting weight in my hand as I swung it in an arc, aiming for the closest monster's left leg. The heavy spiked ball smashed into the limb, and the wood shattered. The creature went down hard.

Next to me, Declan threw a blast of heavenly fire at one on the left, while Connor tried out his potion bombs. They flew as flashes of color and exploded against the trees, causing them to freeze or burst into flame.

The monster that I'd felled was crawling toward me, claws outstretched. I darted around, barely avoiding a slice, and slammed my mace against its head...area. The creature slowed but didn't stop, so I went for each limb with my weapon, trying to smash the beast into oblivion.

Finally, it lay still, then disappeared in a poof of dark magic.

Damn, these things were hard to get rid of.

To my right, Cass and Aidan shifted into their griffin forms. They were massive, with huge beaks and a wingspan that stretched at least fifteen feet across. They launched themselves into the air, heading for the forest beyond the attacking monsters.

Only then did I realize that more of the trees were coming alive.

Shit.

At least four more of them. Then eight. Then twelve.

Oh fates, were there too many of them for us to fight?

15

As more monsters came to life, I joined Nix in her attack against a particularly large tree creature. She wielded an enormous mallet that she'd conjured, slamming it into the beast's limbs. To our right, Claire hurled fireballs at one of the monsters.

Roarke, Del's man, had adopted his demon form. His skin had turned dark gray and his muscles had increased in size, enough that his shirt had disappeared. His dark wings carried him high in the sky, and he dive-bombed one of the monsters, using his massive strength to catch a limb and tear it right off.

Ares the vampire moved so fast that he confused the monster who chased him. He wielded a sword that quickly separated limb from body, and he was onto the next monster within seconds.

Nix and I finally obliterated the tree monster that we fought, and I turned to face the ones that ran toward us.

Too many.

It would take too long to fight them.

"Go!" Connor shouted. "We'll hold them off."

"They'll overrun you!" I shouted.

"Nah." He pointed to Aidan and Ares. "The three of us can hold them off. And if not, I'll hitch a ride on Aidan, and Ares can outrun anything."

It was a good plan, actually. They could distract while we saved Del and Mari.

"I'm fine with it!" Ares's voice carried across the clearing, his advanced hearing having picked up on Connor volunteering them for the job.

Aidan roared, his griffin call cutting through the air.

"That sounds like an affirmative," Connor said, hurling one of his potion bombs at a monster.

The blue glass ball smashed against the creature's chest, splattering it with sparkling liquid. Blue veins shot out from the chest, turning the whole creature to ice. The monster staggered two steps forward, limbs freezing, then crashed to the ground and shattered.

Connor looked at me. "Go! Save your sister."

He didn't have to tell me twice. "Thanks."

I turned and ran, Nix joining me. We headed right for the path that cut through the forest. Claire caught up, along with Declan and Roarke. Cass was the last to follow, flying overhead in her griffin form. She joined us on the ground, shifting as she landed.

Together, we sprinted down the path, leaving the battle behind. Aiden, Ares, and Connor distracted the creatures from following us. The slightest bit of worry tugged at me, but Connor was right. They were strong enough to hold off the monsters. And in a worst-case scenario, they could run for it.

"Do you feel that?" Cass asked from beside me.

Dark magic prickled against my skin, a warning charm that made me shiver. "Yeah."

A second later, we saw it.

A wall of massive orange flame.

The forest path was about to terminate, right into a wall of fire.

The six of us skidded to a halt right before the flame. The wall extended as far as I could see in either direction, blasting my face with heat. I winced, shielding my eyes as I tried to see to the top.

Roarke launched himself into the sky, his dark wings carrying him all the way to the top of the cavern, confirming that there was no way to fly over it. I could hear his frustrated curse from here. Could feel his anxiety for Del. He loved her, and now this damned fire cut him off from saving her. Similar desperation clawed at me. We were getting closer, but our odds were getting worse.

"Shit." Frustration creased Nix's brow. "I can't conjure enough water to deal with this."

Declan approached, his hand outstretched. "You may not need to."

He touched the flame, wincing slightly. Then he stuck his hand right in.

I bit back a cry and resisted the urge to jump forward and yank him away.

He stepped back and showed us his hand, unburned. "Heavenly fire."

"Well that sucks worse." Cass frowned. "Nothing can take out heavenly fire."

"Of course the bastard used heavenly fire," Nix said. "Fucking angels."

I eyed Declan, hope surging in my chest. I knew the rules were different for angels when it came to heavenly fire. He approached the fiery wall again, reaching both hands into it. His magic surged on the air, filling it with the scent of a rainstorm and the sound of a roaring river. I held my breath as he worked.

His white aura glowed brighter, and the fire in front of us started to fade. Just a section of it, but it was enough.

He formed a little portal, and I didn't wait for directions. I just sprinted for it and leapt through, then rolled on the ground on the other side. Fire heated my skin, and my eyes watered.

Shit!

That hurt.

I lurched upright, patting myself off to make sure I wasn't blazing, and darted out of the way so my friends could come through. As they leapt through the portal, I inspected my surroundings.

A massive house sat on a hill about two hundred yards from me. It looked like a freaking haunted mansion. In the perpetual dusk, I expected a lightning bolt to crash behind it.

Nix appeared next to me and gasped. "She's in there!"

"You can feel her now? Both of them?"

She nodded, excitement gleaming on her face. "That barrier of heavenly fire was what blocked my ability to find them. Now that we're on the other side, I can sense them."

"And they're okay?" Roarke asked, desperation making his voice rough.

He hadn't spoken much during this journey, and I realized why. He was barely holding it together. Despite the fact that he'd fought with the skill and viciousness of a seasoned, decorated warrior, he was out of his mind with worry.

Couldn't blame him.

"They're alive," Nix said. "That's all I can feel."

Declan joined us, which meant everyone was through.

"I'm going to use illusion to make us invisible," Cass said. "They won't be able to see us approach. But we won't be able to see each other either. So keep your pace steady, and we'll all group up by that big bush under the window on the left." She pointed to the darkened window and the skeletal bush that sat in front of it.

"Let's go get them," I said.

Once everyone around me disappeared, I looked down at my body. Gone.

Wow. Cool skill.

I set off across the grass at a steady jog, checking out the three-story house as I ran. The haunted house vibe only increased as we neared. Occasionally, I saw people pass in front of the windows. Everyone wore an identical red robe, and eventually, the effect became cultish.

A cult.

The Weeds had said that he'd been hired by a group. Probably a cult, blindly following Acius.

Finally, I reached the bush and pressed myself up against the brick wall. My shoulder hit someone else's, and I nearly jumped.

"Hey," I whispered.

"Hey." Cass's voice came back at me.

"I'm here," Nix said.

After a moment, everyone checked in, and Cass let the magic fade. We all appeared, tucked out of sight at the very bottom of the house. Unless someone walked outside or leaned out of a window, they wouldn't see us.

"Let's go around back. See if there is a quieter entrance." I led the way, and we moved in a silent, single-file line around the edge of the house.

Fortunately, I didn't see a single sign of security anywhere. Acius assumed his giant monsters and wall of fire would keep people out.

Idiot.

At the back of the building, I spotted a root cellar door that was nearly flush against the ground.

Oh, thank fates.

We approached it silently, and to my surprise, it was locked only by a big metal padlock. Roarke reached for it and crushed it in his big gray hand, then tore it away.

"Well, that works," I murmured.

The metal hinges squeaked as Declan and Roarke lifted the two doors. I tensed, waiting for an alarm to sound, but none did.

Fantastic.

I slipped down the stairs, into a long empty room. The packed dirt floor was damp underfoot, and there were no lights in the space. From behind me, one of the FireSouls ignited the magic in her lightstone ring, providing light for the rest of us.

The six of us moved silently to the end of the room, then slipped out the door.

Into chaos.

A group of ten cloaked figures leapt up from where they sat around a table. They turned to us, crimson cloaks flying. I drew a dagger from the ether and hurled it at the nearest figure. The blade sank into his left eye, and he flew backward, crashing into the table and turning it over.

My friends joined the attack, throwing fire and weapons. But we were too slow. One of the figures in the back set up an alarm, pressing a lever on the wall that made a siren wail.

"Shit." Cass spun to face us. "Get out of here. Go find them. We'll hold these ones off."

She was right. With the alarm sounded, forces would rally, and some would go toward the prisoners.

I sprinted away, Nix and Roarke on my heels. Declan stayed behind with Cass and Claire, fending off the remaining red cloaks.

The three of us sprinted out of the room and down a wide hall. It was empty and windowless, with old yellow bulbs in the ceiling for light.

"Where is she?" I asked Nix, praying that her dragon sense would work.

"Straight ahead and to the right."

We ran full tilt, not bothering to silence our footsteps. I drew my sword from the ether, gripping the hilt tight as I ran.

Footsteps thundered above us as troops rallied. Was Acius here now? Would I get to face him?

Grim hope swelled in my chest. I hoped so. I wanted to take the bastard out, once and for all.

We hit the end of the hall and turned right, sprinting toward a man at the end.

"A guard," Nix said. "They're behind that door."

Roarke put on a burst of speed and raced into the lead. The guard turned to face him, his hand raised. He threw a blast of blue energy at Roarke, but missed when Roarke dodged. Before the guard could power up another blast, Roarke reached him and grabbed his head. He grunted as he tore it right off his body. Blood sprayed, but Roarke didn't seem to care. He didn't even dodge the spray, just tossed the head and turned to the door, crashing through it.

"Not much for subtlety, is he?" I asked Nix, almost giddy at the idea of finally seeing Mari.

"Not when Del is at risk."

We sprinted into the room behind him. Immediately, I felt the charm that bound my magic. Just like at the prison. No wonder Del and Mari hadn't been able to escape.

As soon as I saw Mari, my heart dropped. She lay on the ground, her eyes closed. Roarke had swooped up Del, who looked worse for wear. But she hadn't been hit with the same curse as Mari.

I fell to my knees at Mari's side. Her black makeup was smudged and nearly gone, her skin so pale she looked nearly transparent.

Gently, I touched her shoulder. "Mari. Mari!"

She opened her eyes. Pain gleamed in their depths. Immediately, I realized she hadn't gotten to take the second dose of the antidote like I had. She was nearly gone.

I drew my potion bag from the ether and scrambled around inside, looking for the pep-up potion that Connor had given me. It wouldn't fix her, but it would give her a bit of strength.

Vaguely, I was aware of Roarke, Del, and Nix going to guard the door as I poured the potion down Mari's throat. She sputtered and gasped, but managed to swallow most of it.

"Are you okay?" I asked.

"Peachy." Her voice was barely a croak, and my heart twisted. The damned fallen angel had better have a cure here. It was our only hope. We'd bet *everything* on it.

"Does he have a cure?" I was so scared I could barely speak the words.

She nodded, grimacing. "Promised it if I gave him your location."

"You should have!"

She gave a weak laugh.

"I can find the cure," Nix said from the doorway. The sound of a fight outside indicated that Roarke and Del were holding someone off. "I feel it. On the top floor, to the left. Probably in a lab or something."

"Let's go get it." I reached for Mari. "Let me help you stand."

She rose slowly to her feet, agony evident in every motion. She must have caught sight of the worry on my face, because she said, "Hey, I'm doing great compared to earlier."

I helped her stagger to the door, and realized that we weren't going to get anywhere fast. Not as fast as we needed to, at least. Mari was just too weak. We couldn't leave her, though. Not with the alert sounded.

"Roarke!" Nix cried.

He appeared in the doorway, his gaze going straight to Mari. He got the clue immediately, and raced to her side. "I'm going to pick you up, okay?"

Mari grimaced, then nodded.

Roarke swooped her into his arms, and we hurried from the room. In the hallway, Del had turned incorporeal, her blue Phantom form shining bright as one of the guards swiped at her with his huge blade.

It passed right through her, and she didn't even flinch. A half second later, she turned corporeal again and sliced her sword through the man's middle. She grunted as the blade cut through, then returned to her Phantom form.

"Let's go," Nix shouted. "I know where the antidote is."

Thank fates for FireSouls.

Together, we sprinted down the hall and found the stairs. I led the charge, taking the stairs two at a time until I reached the top floor. I pushed open the door as quietly as I could manage.

The hall was empty.

Hell yeah.

We sprinted out, and I darted to the side, allowing the Fire-Souls to take the lead so they could take us to the antidote.

Nix and Del raced toward the end of the hall and turned right into a room. I ran in after them, immediately spotting the tables full of potion bottles and ingredients.

Oh, thank fates.

Nix raced toward one of the tables and grabbed up two blue bottles. "This is it. I can feel it."

I yanked the bottles from her and hurried toward Mari, who was still in Roarke's arms, looking like something the cat had dragged in. I pulled the cap off one tiny bottle and held it to her lips.

She drank, then glared at me, her color already improved as she scrambled out of Roarke's arms. "Now take yours!"

"I will!" I reached for the cork.

Something slammed into me before I could open the vial. I flew backward and crashed into the table behind me, pain exploding within me. The tiny glass vessel that I'd been holding flew through the air. It felt like an electric shock had lit me up from within.

Despite the pain, I reached out for the antidote. Desperation stabbed me in the chest when I heard it shatter.

I could imagine the cure splashing uselessly against the wooden floor.

I scrambled upright, pain surging through my body. Through bleary eyes, I spotted Acius.

It had to be him. He had the electric power—the one that had put black burn marks all over The Weeds.

His ragged wings flared behind him, black feathers tipped in white. Only now did I realize that the white was damage from when he'd fallen. From the flame I'd seen in the painting.

He was tall and gaunt, but the aura of power that surged from him was enormous. He was in the room in the blink of an eye, a horde of his minions following.

Del, Nix, and Roarke charged the enemy forces, colliding with them in a blast of blood and magic.

It was chaos. Battle erupted in the small room, fire and ice flashing as mages shot their worst. Blood sprayed from Roarke's claws, while Nix and Del fought like banshees. Del turned incorporeal immediately, her shining blue form dancing through the room, hair swinging as she turned corporeal long enough for her blade to slice through a red cloak. Nix fought with her massive mallet, doing enough damage that no one got close to her. Wally had shown up, and he was busy lighting a red cloak on fire.

I called on my mace, surging to my feet and charging for Acius.

Visions of Mari flashed in my mind, and rage like I'd never known filled me. This bastard was responsible for everything.

He laughed as he saw me coming. "I hoped you'd come to me."

"You're going to regret that." I swung my mace at him, and he dodged, shooting another blast of electricity at me.

I darted left, but it plowed into my side. Pain shot through me, my muscles seizing, and I flew backward and smashed into the wall.

I staggered upright, but he was already turning to throw a blast of electricity at Nix. She took a hit to the right arm and tumbled backward.

Damn, this guy was too fast. Too strong.

I climbed to my feet and charged him, lengthening the chain on my mace so I could hit him from farther away. The heavy metal ball smashing into his arm, and he roared.

Instead of going down like I'd expected him to, he managed to stay on his feet and turned to face me. I conjured my shield just in time, going for a wooden one I had stashed in the ether for lightning fights. The electric shock that he sent toward me slammed into it. The force shoved me back against the wall.

I went down hard, crashing onto my butt. Normally I might be able to hold my ground, but between my weakness from the fire veins curse and Acius's electric magic, I couldn't keep up. He was going to kill me before the curse ever had a chance.

It took everything I had to stagger upright, all of me aching. As soon as I gained my feet, I caught sight of Declan surging through the door. Determination set his brow, and he headed straight for Acius, his blade raised.

Mari appeared at my side, dropping to her knees. She shoved something at me. "Here, drink this!"

I looked at her, shocked.

"It's the antidote. I found another." She held up an identical vial. "Take it!"

I grabbed it from her and swigged it back. A faintly floral taste hit me, then the fire in my veins faded. Within seconds, it was gone. Strength surged through me.

"Amazing, right?" she said.

"Totally amazing." I'd known I was growing weaker, but not *how* much weaker.

I leapt upright, and she followed.

We turned toward the battle. The room was nearly full— Cass, Claire, and Roarke had joined us, along with at least twenty of Acius's minions. Quarters were too close for Mari's bow, so she drew a sword and dived into the fray.

We were outnumbered but not overpowered. Acius's cult members were strong, but nothing compared to us. He was the only one who would be an issue.

I raced for Acius, drawing a dagger from the ether. He and Declan were engaged in a sword fight that moved so fast I could barely see their blades.

When Acius's back was to me, I hurled the dagger right at him. The steel sank into his left side, directly under the wing. He roared and turned, his sights landing on me.

Before I could so much as twitch, he threw a blast of electric energy at me. It slammed right into my chest, bowling me backward. I crashed into the wall, annoyance and pain surging through me.

Declan attacked him from behind, drawing his ire. Acius turned from me. I sucked in a painful breath and pushed myself off the floor, managing to stagger to my feet.

All around us, the tide of the battle was turning in our favor. When Connor, Aidan, and Ares appeared in the door, I knew we had the red cloaks beat. We'd just have to team up on Acius.

Long-range attacks were best for him, and I needed something original. Something he wouldn't see coming. Because clearly, weapons weren't working.

Declan fought him in front of a huge stained glass window, a violent tableau of two angels at war.

Quickly, I sliced my thumb with my finger, letting blood well. I called upon my dragon blood, imagining a new magic. A power I'd never used before. I'd witnessed a witch use it once and thought I could replicate it.

I crept toward Acius, careful to stay out of his line of sight, then raised my hand to my mouth. I blew across my palm like I was blowing Acius a kiss.

Pale white smoke drifted off my palm, and I whispered, "Sleep. Weaken."

The smoke drifted over Acius, and he stiffened, swaying. He turned to me, his eyes widening as he saw me lower my palm. Understanding flickered in his eyes, and he mouthed the word, "Dragon Blood."

Shock lanced me. I lunged for him.

Acius stumbled backward, my magic weakening his muscles as exhaustion dragged at him. Slowed him. Declan was moving in for the kill, but I got there first.

I gripped Acius's neck, choking him. I pushed him against the wall. He was weak from the sleep magic, but I made sure to feed my nullification power into him. No way I'd let him blast me with his electric power. I could feel it fighting inside him, though, trying to burst free and zap me.

"What do you know about me?"

"Dragon Blood. Your signature—it's so strong. You've made much magic, haven't you?"

The question made horror slash through me.

What I've always feared.

That I'd make so much new magic I wouldn't be able to control my signature and someone clever would figure it out.

It would be the end of me.

He grinned widely, delight shining in his weary eyes. "Join me, Dragon Blood. Together we can do great things." Weakly, he gestured to the people beyond me. "We'll evict them from Magic's Bend and take it for our own. It's the perfect city—protected from humans, hidden from the world. It should be darker. The residents of Grimrealm should move to the surface. Join me."

His magic reached to me, darkness and power. He was trying to convince me to be on his side, using whatever snake-oil salesman gift he had.

To join him.

Hell no.

He had some kind of magic that pulled at me, because there was *no way* I'd ever want to join him. It was my job to protect Magic's Bend, and I loved it. I *believed* in it. I'd been born a Dragon Blood, and it'd led me to my sacred duty—to protect Magic's Bend as a Demon Slayer. This guy was just getting in my way. Another job to be done.

The most dangerous job I'd ever faced—but a job nonetheless.

"Why did you poison my sister and me?" I demanded.

"You stood in our way." He smiled, as if he were complimenting me. I could feel his electric magic pulsing inside him. I fought to push more of my nullification magic into him, but I was flagging. He was too strong. "You foiled us both times, so I had to get rid of you." He shook his head. "But no, I was wrong. You have proved to be so much more. With you, we can accomplish anything. Join us. I'll make you a queen."

Queen.

That had its appeal, but not if it came from him.

"Ew. *No.*" I shook him, conjuring a dagger. I had my answers. It was time to end this.

Acius's eyes flicked to the dagger in my hand. Disappointment welled in their depths. "I hoped I'd had you. You would be perfect with me."

"Never."

I raised the dagger.

His magic burst out of him, an electric shock so strong that it threw me backward. I slammed into the wall, realizing that he'd probably been holding back. As soon as he'd realized what I was, he'd wanted to talk to me.

To try to convince me.

Aching, I started to drag myself up. Declan lunged for Acius.

But the fallen angel was too fast. He put on a burst of speed and plowed through the stained glass. It shattered in a riot of color, and he fell.

I sprinted to the window and looked down. He'd already had his wings out when he was fighting, and they spread wide, helping him surge on a current of air and fly high into the sky.

Next to me, Declan's wings flared wide, and he leapt out the window, racing for Acius. Roarke sprinted by me, jumping out the window as well, taking off into the dark cavern.

Through the gloom, I could see Acius dig into his pocket.

No!

"A transport charm!" I shouted.

He hurled the red object to the ground. Red?

Transport charms weren't red.

It shattered, sending streaks of red electric light shooting right for me. I dived left, skidding on the ground. Out of the corner of my eye, I caught sight of the crimson light shooting toward the red cloaks. Ten of them still fought my friends. A sharp beam hit each of them, and they disappeared.

I scrambled through the shards of broken glass, not feeling the cuts, as I raced to see if Acius was gone.

When I looked out into the gloomy cavern, I saw only Declan and Roarke.

"He escaped." Frustration welled inside me, nearly exploding in my chest. I surged to my feet, wanting to scream. "That bastard escaped!"

"And he took his minions with him." Mari nudged a fallen red cloak with her toe. "The living ones, at least."

I heaved a sigh and leaned against the wall. The sight of Mari reminded me of everything that had been at stake just fifteen minutes ago.

She'd been nearly dead.

I'd been close on her heels.

I staggered to her and wrapped my arms around her, focusing on the win. Because this *was* a win.

"Thank fates we were in time," I said.

She hugged me. "It was close. I'm not going to lie."

"No kidding. You looked like death warmed over." I pulled back and met her eyes. "Thanks for finding the antidote. I thought I was a goner."

She smiled. "I was scared there for a bit."

The word "scared" made a memory flare in my mind. I leaned close and whispered, "He called me Dragon Blood. I've made so much new magic that he sensed my signature."

"Bastard." Despair flashed on Mari's face. "What will he do with that knowledge?"

Fear chilled me. "I don't know."

If he wasn't trying to convert me to his side, to use me, would he rat me out?

But who would believe him?

Fates, I prayed he didn't know about Mari. I had to believe he only knew about me. I had so much more new magic. Magic whose signature I hadn't learned how to control. And I'd created the brief bit of sleep magic in front of him.

I turned to face the room, realizing that Cass, Del, and Nix were standing close enough to hear.

They know what I am.

The three shrugged.

"Doesn't matter to us," Cass said.

"Be a bit hypocritical if it did." Nix laughed.

Shock raced through me. The secret that I'd kept for so long was out. A combo of exhaustion and rage had made us unwary.

"I'm, ah—" I didn't know what to say. I felt like I should apologize for keeping the secret at all. Part of me stood by my decision. But another part...

I liked the FireSouls.

I'd known for a long time I should have trusted them.

I just...hadn't. Not enough. Which was my own fault.

"Don't worry about it," Del said. "You look like you're about to apologize or something, and...well, don't."

She knew what I was going to say before I even said it. Because she'd been me, once. Hiding secrets from her friends. Feeling guilty about it.

"Yeah," Cass added. "We've got your back. No explanations needed."

Nix nodded her agreement.

Something loosened in my chest. A feeling of lightness came over me. Almost like freedom.

I'd always figured it was no harm done to keep this secret from our friends. That it was better this way. Safer.

It hadn't been.

My fear had held me back, and I hadn't even realized it. A weight had been lifted from my shoulders, and it was awesome.

"Thanks." I looked at Mari, glad to see that she didn't look freaked out either. They didn't necessarily know about her, but it would be easy for them to assume. They'd seen us both in action many times and knew how similar we were.

Probably easy for Acius to figure it out too, but I wouldn't dwell on that. Not yet.

Declan and Roarke returned to the room, flying back through the broken window. Claire, Connor, Aires, and Aiden were rifling through the bodies of the fallen, no doubt looking for clues about what the hell was going on. Wally was eating a red cloak's soul.

Reality called.

I turned back to everyone. "Let's search the place. Because this isn't over. Not by a long shot."

EPILOGUE

THE NEXT DAY, I SAT IN POTIONS & PASTILLES, A PROPER MARTINI in my hand. Finally, a good drink. Even better, I wasn't wearing my ghost suit.

Instead, I wore my usual white silk pants and top with my hair properly washed and flowing over my shoulders in a smooth wave. No knots here.

It was the little things in life that kept a person feeling human.

Like the memory of Acius's mansion ablaze.

I closed my eyes and savored the memory as I sipped the chilled martini. I could almost feel the heat of it on my face again. It drove away the fear and anger that he'd figured out what I was because I'd made to much new magic lately.

I'd been foolish. I'd needed that power, but still...

My actions had revealed me.

No. Focus on the victory.

Acius might have escaped, but after we'd searched the place, I'd lit his house up like a Fourth of July bonfire. His headquarters were toast, and we'd gotten all the evidence we could. There hadn't been much of it, but we'd use it to hunt him down like the rat he was.

"You okay?" Mari's voice sounded from above me, and I opened my eyes to see her sit down next to me.

She was dressed in her usual Elvira getup, with her sweep of black makeup and black bouffant. She had a Manhattan in hand, and the dark crimson liquid looked almost like blood.

"I'm great. Just reliving the blaze."

"Bastard deserved it." She shook her head. "Trying to take over Magic's Bend. What a prick."

"We'll stop him," I said. "He tried to get rid of us, but he'll never manage it."

Only now, he wanted to use me more than he wanted to get rid of me.

I'd never let him. I'd die first. *He'd* die first.

Mari shook her head. "The idiot doesn't realize there are plenty of people to pick up the job if he actually did manage to take us out."

And she was right. The FireSouls would fight for Magic's Bend. Declan would. Even our friends in Scotland at the Undercover Protectorate.

Taking us out wouldn't do a bit of good for him.

Not that I'd let him.

She reached for my hand and squeezed. "He may know what you are. Maybe me too. But we'll deal with him. Like we deal with everything."

I squeezed her hand back and nodded.

I sipped my martini again and looked around at the small crowd in Potions & Pastilles. Everyone was there—all the Fire-Souls and their guys, Connor and Claire. Even Aethelred the seer.

We hadn't spoken about our true natures with the FireSouls again, but I felt more relaxed around them. It was weird, but nice. And we were here to celebrate our victory over Acius. It wasn't a full victory—that would deserve a bigger party—but we had to take the good things in life while we could get them.

Because I was sure that bad news was coming from his quarter. There was no way he'd just disappear now. We'd pissed him off good and proper—*and* he knew that Mari and I were Dragon Bloods.

I shivered and pushed the thought away.

Across from me, Mari looked toward the door. Her brows rose. I turned to see Declan entering.

My breath caught. He was dressed in all black, his fallen angel beauty a contrast for his rugged form. He looked damned good.

As usual.

He looked right at me, and I smiled.

When I turned back to Mari, she was gone.

Declan took her seat. "You look beautiful."

"Thanks. I clean up pretty nice. So do you."

He grinned.

"So, uh." I searched for the words I wanted to say. "This thing between us. I thought I'd give it a try."

"I thought that's what we've been doing?"

"Well..." He'd been doing it, maybe. I'd been hiding behind my nullification magic and any excuse I could get to avoid growing close. "I'm going to try. I've been practicing controlling my nullification magic."

"Thanks." He smiled. "I'd take you even if you couldn't control it, you know."

A warm flush of pleasure suffused me. He wanted to be with me *even if* I made him physically ill.

He must really like me.

Wild.

"I'm going to get a drink," he said, acting like this whole

getting close thing was totally normal. It probably was—to him. Maybe it would be for me, too. One day.

"I'll be right back." He got up and went to the bar.

I sipped my drink and watched him walk away, wondering where this whole thing was going between us. If I survived Acius and all the threats he posed, I knew I wanted to find out.

THANK YOU FOR READING!

I hope you enjoyed reading this book as much as I enjoyed writing it. Reviews are *so* helpful to authors. I really appreciate all reviews, both positive and negative. If you want to leave one, you can do so on Amazon or GoodReads.

If you'd like to learn a little more about the FireSouls (Cass, Nix, and Del), you can join my mailing list at www.linseyhall.com/subscribe to get a free ebook copy of *Hidden Magic*, a story of their early adventures. Turn the page for an excerpt.

EXCERPT OF HIDDEN MAGIC

Jungle, Southeast Asia
  Five years before the events in Ancient Magic

"How much are we being paid for this job again?" I glanced at the dudes filling the bar. It was a motley crowd of supernaturals, many of whom looked shifty as hell.

"Not nearly enough for one as dangerous as this." Del frowned at the man across the bar, who was giving her his best sexy face. There was a lot of eyebrow movement happening. "Is he having a seizure?"

"Looks like it." Nix grinned. "Though I gotta say, I wasn't expecting this. We're basically in a tree, for magic's sake. In the middle of the jungle! Where are all these dudes coming from?"

"According to my info, there's a mining operation near here. Though I'd say we're more *under* a tree than *in* a tree."

"I'm with Cass," Del said. "Under, not in."

"Fair enough," Nix said.

We were deep in Southeast Asia, in a bar that had long ago been reclaimed by the jungle. A massive fig tree had grown over and around the ancient building, its huge roots strangling the stone walls. It was straight out of a fairy tale.

Monks had once lived here, but a few supernaturals of indeterminate species had gotten ahold of it and turned it into a watering hole for the local supernaturals. We were meeting our contact here, but he was late.

"Hey, pretty lady." A smarmy voice sounded from my left. "What are you?"

I turned to face the guy who was giving me the up and down, his gaze roving from my tank top to my shorts. He wasn't Clarence, our local contact. And if he meant "what kind of supernatural are you?" I sure as hell wouldn't be answering. That could get me killed.

"Not interested is what I am," I said.

"Aww, that's no way to treat a guy." He grabbed my hip, rubbed his thumb up and down.

I smacked his hand away, tempted to throat-punch him. It was my favorite move, but I didn't want to start a fight before Clarence got here. Didn't want to piss off our boss.

The man raised his hands. "Hey, hey. No need to get feisty. You three sisters?"

I glanced at Nix and Del, at their dark hair that was so different from my red. We were all about twenty, but we looked nothing alike. And while we might call ourselves sisters—*deirfiúr* in our native Irish—this idiot didn't know that.

"Go away." I had no patience for dirt bags who touched me without asking. "Run along and flirt with your hand, because that's all the action you'll be getting tonight."

His face turned a mottled red, and he raised a fist. His magic welled, the scent of rotten fruit overwhelming.

He thought he was going to smack me? Or use his magic against me?

Ha.

I lashed out, punching him in the throat. His eyes bulged and he gagged. I kneed him in the crotch, grinning when he keeled over.

"Hey!" A burly man with a beard lunged for us, his buddy beside him following. "That's no way—"

"To treat a guy?" I finished for him as I kicked out at him. My tall, heavy boots collided with his chest, sending him flying backward. I never used my magic—didn't want to go to jail and didn't want to blow things up—but I sure as hell could fight.

His friend raised his hand and sent a blast of wind at us. It threw me backward, sending me skidding across the floor.

By the time I'd scrambled to my feet, a brawl had broken out in the bar. Fists flew left and right, with a bit of magic thrown in. Nothing bad enough to ruin the bar, like jets of flame, because no one wanted to destroy the only watering hole for a hundred miles, but enough that it lit up the air with varying magical signatures.

Nix conjured a baseball bat and swung it at a burly guy who charged her, while Del teleported behind a horned demon and smashed a chair over his head. I'd always been jealous of Del's ability to sneak up on people like that.

All in all, it was turning into a good evening. A fight between supernaturals was fun.

"Enough!" the bartender bellowed. "Or no more beer!"

The patrons quieted immediately. Fights might be fun, but they weren't worth losing beer over.

I glared at the jerk who'd started it. There was no way I'd take the blame, even though I'd thrown the first punch. He should have known better.

The bartender gave me a look and I shrugged, hiking a thumb at the jerk who'd touched me. "He shoulda kept his hands to himself."

"Fair enough," the bartender said.

I nodded and turned to find Nix and Del. They'd grabbed our beers and were putting them on a table in the corner. I went to join them.

We were a team. Sisters by choice, ever since we'd woken in a field at fifteen with no memories other than those that said we were FireSouls on the run from someone who had hurt us. Who was hunting us.

Our biggest goal, even bigger than getting out from under our current boss's thumb, was to save enough money to buy concealment charms that would hide us from the monster who hunted us. He was just a shadowy memory, but it was enough to keep us running.

"Where is Clarence, anyway?" I pulled my damp tank top away from my sweaty skin. The jungle was damned hot. We couldn't break into the temple until Clarence gave us the information we needed to get past the guard at the front. And we didn't need to spend too much longer in this bar.

Del glanced at her watch, her blue eyes flashing with annoyance. "He's twenty minutes late. Old Man Bastard said he should be here at eight."

Old Man Bastard—OMB for short—was our boss. His name said it all. Del, Nix, and I were FireSouls, the most despised species of supernatural because we could steal other magical being's powers if we killed them. We'd never done that, of course, but OMB didn't care. He'd figured out our secret when we were too young to hide it effectively and had been blackmailing us to work for him ever since.

It'd been four years of finding and stealing treasure on his behalf. Treasure hunting was our other talent, a gift from the dragon with whom legend said we shared a soul. No one had seen a dragon in centuries, so I wasn't sure if the legend was even true, but dragons were covetous, so it made sense they had a knack for finding treasure.

"What are we after again?" Nix asked.

"A pair of obsidian daggers," Del said. "Nice ones."

"And how much is this job worth?" Nix repeated my earlier question. Money was always on our minds. It was our only chance at buying our freedom, but OMB didn't pay us enough for it to be feasible anytime soon. We kept meticulous track of our earnings and saved like misers anyway.

"A thousand each."

"Damn, that's pathetic." I slouched back in my chair and stared up at the ceiling, too bummed about our crappy pay to even be impressed by the stonework and vines above my head.

"Hey, pretty ladies." The oily voice made my skin crawl. We just couldn't get a break in here. I looked up to see Clarence, our contact.

Clarence was a tall man, slender as a vine, and had the slicked back hair and pencil-thin mustache of a 1940s movie star. Unfortunately, it didn't work on him. Probably because his stare was like a lizard's. He was more Gomez Addams than Clark Gable. I'd bet anything that he liked working for OMB.

"Hey, Clarence," I said. "Pull up a seat and tell us how to get into the temple."

Clarence slid into a chair, his movement eerily snakelike. I shivered and scooted my chair away, bumping into Del. The scent of her magic flared, a clean hit of fresh laundry, as she no doubt suppressed her instinct to transport away from Clarence. If I had her gift of teleportation, I'd have to repress it as well.

"How about a drink first?" Clarence said.

Del growled, but Nix interjected, her voice almost nice. She had the most self control out of the three of us. "No can do, Clarence. You know... Mr. Oribis"—her voice tripped on the name, probably because she wanted to call him OMB—"wants the daggers soon. Maybe next time, though."

"Next time." Clarence shook his head like he didn't believe

her. He might be a snake, but he was a clever one. His chest puffed up a bit. "You know I'm the only one who knows how to get into the temple. How to get into any of the places in this jungle."

"And we're so grateful you're meeting with us. Mr. Oribis is so grateful." Nix dug into her pocket and pulled out the crumpled envelope that contained Clarence's pay. We'd counted it and found—unsurprisingly—that it was more than ours combined, even though all he had to do was chat with us for two minutes. I'd wanted to scream when I'd seen it.

Clarence's gaze snapped to the money. "All right, all right."

Apparently his need to be flattered went out the window when cash was in front of his face. Couldn't blame him, though. I was the same way.

"So, what are we up against?" I asked.

The temple containing the daggers had been built by supernaturals over a thousand years ago. Like other temples of its kind, it was magically protected. Clarence's intel would save us a ton of time and damage to the temple if we could get around the enchantments rather than breaking through them.

"Dvarapala. A big one."

"A gatekeeper?" I'd seen one of the giant, stone monster statues at another temple before.

"Yep." He nodded slowly. "Impossible to get through. The temple's as big as the Titanic—hidden from humans, of course —but no one's been inside in centuries, they say."

Hidden from humans was a given. They had no idea supernaturals existed, and we wanted to keep it that way.

"So how'd you figure out the way in?" Del asked. "And why *haven't* you gone in? Bet there's lots of stuff you could fence in there. Temples are usually full of treasure."

"A bit of pertinent research told me how to get in. And I'd

rather sell the entrance information and save my hide. It won't be easy to get past the booby traps in there."

Hide? Snakeskin, more like. Though he had a point. I didn't think he'd last long trying to get through a temple on his own.

"So? Spill it," I said, anxious to get going.

He leaned in, and the overpowering scent of cologne and sweat hit me. I grimaced, held my breath, then leaned forward to hear his whispers.

As soon as Clarence walked away, the communications charms around my neck vibrated. I jumped, then groaned. Only one person had access to this charm.

I shoved the small package Clarence had given me into my short's pocket and pressed my fingertips to the comms charm, igniting its magic.

"Hello, Mr. Oribis." I swallowed my bile at having to be polite.

"Girls," he grumbled.

Nix made a gagging face. We hated when he called us girls.

"Change of plans. You need to go to the temple tonight."

"What? But it's dark. We're going tomorrow." He never changed the plans on us. This was weird.

"I need the daggers sooner. Go tonight."

My mind raced. "The jungle is more dangerous in the dark. We'll do it if you pay us more."

"Twice the usual," Del said.

A tinny laugh echoed from the charm. "Pay *you* more? You're lucky I pay you at all."

I gritted my teeth and said, "But we've been working for you for four years without a raise."

"And you'll be working for me for four more years. And four

after that. And four after that." Annoyance lurked in his tone. So did his low opinion of us.

Del's and Nix's brows crinkled in distress. We'd always suspected that OMB wasn't planning to let us buy our freedom, but he'd dangled that carrot in front of us. What he'd just said made that seem like a big fat lie, though. One we could add to the many others he'd told us.

An urge to rebel, to stand up to the bully who controlled our lives, seethed in my chest.

"No," I said. "You treat us like crap, and I'm sick of it. Pay us fairly."

"I treat you like *crap,* as you so eloquently put it, because that is exactly what you are. *FireSouls.*" He spit the last word, imbuing it with so much venom I thought it might poison me.

I flinched, frantically glancing around to see if anyone in the bar had heard what he'd called us. Fortunately, they were all distracted. That didn't stop my heart from thundering in my ears as rage replaced the fear. I opened my mouth to shout at him, but snapped it shut. I was too afraid of pissing him off.

"Get it by dawn," he barked. "Or I'm turning one of you in to the Order of the Magica. Prison will be the least of your worries. They might just execute you."

I gasped. "You wouldn't." Our government hunted and imprisoned—or destroyed—FireSouls.

"Oh, I would. And I'd enjoy it. The three of you have been more trouble than you're worth. You're getting cocky, thinking you have a say in things like this. Get the daggers by dawn, or one of you ends up in the hands of the Order."

My skin chilled, and the floor felt like it had dropped out from under me. He was serious.

"Fine." I bit off the end of the word, barely keeping my voice from shaking. "We'll do it tonight. Del will transport them to you as soon as we have them."

"Excellent." Satisfaction rang in his tone, and my skin crawled. "Don't disappoint me, or you know what will happen."

The magic in the charm died. He'd broken the connection.

I collapsed back against the chair. In times like these, I wished I had it in me to kill. Sure, I offed demons when they came at me on our jobs, but that was easy because they didn't actually die. Killing their earthly bodies just sent them back to their hell.

But I couldn't kill another supernatural. Not even OMB. It might get us out of this lifetime of servitude, but I didn't have it in me. And what if I failed? I was too afraid of his rage—and the consequences—if I didn't succeed.

"Shit, shit, shit." Nix's green eyes were stark in her pale face. "He means it."

"Yeah." Del's voice shook. "We need to get those daggers."

"Now," I said.

"I wish I could just conjure a forgery," Nix said. "I really don't want to go out into the jungle tonight. Getting past the Dvarapala in the dark will suck."

Nix was a conjurer, able to create almost anything using just her magic. Massive or complex things, like airplanes or guns, were outside of her ability, but a couple of daggers wouldn't be hard.

Trouble was, they were a magical artifact, enchanted with the ability to return to whoever had thrown them. Like boomerangs. Though Nix could conjure the daggers, we couldn't enchant them.

"We need to go. We only have six hours until dawn." I grabbed my short swords from the table and stood, shoving them into the holsters strapped to my back.

A hush descended over the crowded bar.

I stiffened, but the sound of the staticky TV in the corner made me relax. They weren't interested in me. Just the news, which was probably being routed through a dozen techno-witches to get this far into the jungle.

The grave voice of the female reporter echoed through the quiet bar. "The FireSoul was apprehended outside of his apartment in Magic's Bend, Oregon. He is currently in the custody of the Order of the Magica, and his trial is scheduled for tomorrow morning. My sources report that execution is possible."

I stifled a crazed laugh. Perfect timing. Just what we needed to hear after OMB's threat. A reminder of what would happen if he turned us into the Order of the Magica. The hush that had descended over the previously rowdy crowd—the kind of hush you get at the scene of a big accident—indicated what an interesting freaking topic this was. FireSouls were the bogeymen. *I* was the bogeyman, even though I didn't use my powers. But as long as no one found out, we were safe.

My gaze darted to Del and Nix. They nodded toward the door. It was definitely time to go.

As the newscaster turned her report toward something more boring and the crowd got rowdy again, we threaded our way between the tiny tables and chairs.

I shoved the heavy wooden door open and sucked in a breath of sticky jungle air, relieved to be out of the bar. Night creatures screeched, and moonlight filtered through the trees above. The jungle would be a nice place if it weren't full of things that wanted to kill us.

"We're never escaping him, are we?" Nix said softly.

"We will." Somehow. Someday. "Let's just deal with this for now."

We found our motorcycles, which were parked in the lot with a dozen other identical ones. They were hulking beasts with massive, all-terrain tires meant for the jungle floor. We'd done a lot of work in Southeast Asia this year, and these were our favored forms of transportation in this part of the world.

Del could transport us, but it was better if she saved her power. It wasn't infinite, though it did regenerate. But we'd learned a long time ago to save Del's power for our escape. Nothing worse than being trapped in a temple with pissed off guardians and a few tripped booby traps.

We'd scouted out the location of the temple earlier that day, so we knew where to go.

I swung my leg over Secretariat—I liked to name my vehicles —and kicked the clutch. The engine roared to life. Nix and Del followed, and we peeled out of the lot, leaving the dingy yellow light of the bar behind.

Our headlights illuminated the dirt road as we sped through the night. Huge fig trees dotted the path on either side, their twisted trunks and roots forming an eerie corridor. Elephant-ear sized leaves swayed in the wind, a dark emerald that gleamed in the light.

Jungle animals howled, and enormous lightning bugs flitted along the path. They were too big to be regular bugs, so they were most likely some kind of fairy, but I wasn't going to stop to investigate. There were dangerous creatures in the jungle at night—one of the reasons we hadn't wanted to go now—and in our world, fairies could be considered dangerous.

Especially if you called them lightning bugs.

A roar sounded in the distance, echoing through the jungle and making the leaves rustle on either side as small animals scurried for safety.

The roar came again, only closer.

Then another, and another.

"Oh shit," I muttered. This was bad.

~~~

Join my mailing list at www.linseyhall.com/subscribe and get a free ebook copy of *Hidden Magic.*

AUTHOR'S NOTE

Thank you for reading *Demon Curse!* If you have read any of my other books, you might be familiar with the fact that I like to include historical places and mythological elements. I always discuss them in the author's note.

The exterior of the supernatural version of the Louvre is based upon the exterior of Notre Dame cathedral, which partially burned while I was writing this book. The graveyards in GrimRealm where the team accessed Acius's hideout are based upon the famous ones in New Orleans—specifically the above ground mausoleums.

The prison where Acius was held was inspired by the famous Chateau D'If, a medieval fortress turned prison located off the south coast of France, near Marsielle. It is a real place, built between 1521-31, and was also a setting in the book The Count of Monte Cristo, written by Alexandre Dumas. There is actually a well inside the prison (which looks more like an old castle) but it's highly doubtful you can climb up into the prison through it. The location in the middle of the sea, combined with the strong currents, makes it incredibly difficult to escape from.

A bit like medieval Alcatraz, though it is now a historical site instead of a prison.

I think that's it for the history and mythology in *Demon Curse* —at least the big things. I hope you enjoyed the book and will come back for more of the FireSouls and Dragon Gods's worlds.

ACKNOWLEDGMENTS

Thank you, Ben, for everything. There would be no books without you.

Thank you to Jena O'Connor and Lindsey Loucks for your excellent editing. The book is immensely better because of you! Thank you Eleonora, Richard, and Aisha for you helpful comments about typos.

Thank you to Orina Kafe for the beautiful cover art.

ABOUT LINSEY

Before becoming a writer, Linsey Hall was a nautical archaeologist who studied shipwrecks from Hawaii and the Yukon to the UK and the Mediterranean. She credits fantasy and historical romances with her love of history and her career as an archaeologist. After a decade of tromping around the globe in search of old bits of stuff that people left lying about, she settled down and started penning her own romance novels. Her Dragon's Gift series draws upon her love of history and the paranormal elements that she can't help but include.

COPYRIGHT

Made in the USA
Monee, IL
12 November 2020

47356968R00127